What People Are Saying ......

One Man Down and Other Titles by the Author

Pearl has written a very funny and compelling page-turner. 11 out of 10!
Jeremy Dein, KC and presenter of the BBC's award-winning series *Murder, Mystery and My Family*

Alex Pearl breaks all the rules of fashionable modern fiction — meaning that his stories are compelling, his characters are plausible and live in a recognisable world, and his writing is clear, vivid and entertaining.
Jonathan Margolis, columnist and author

Alex Pearl's new novel is a highly entertaining tale of shenanigans and skulduggery set in 1980s London ad land. Pearl is a very funny writer, with a keen eye for the absurdities of life.
Ian Critchley, book reviewer and writer

Many a true word is spoken in jest. And former ad man Alex Pearl gives us plenty of pithy truths, as well as spot-on jests, in this witty exposé of the world of advertising agencies in the supercool '80s. Clever, unsparing, engaging and a lot of fun.
Sue Clark, former comedy writer for the BBC and author of *Note to Boy* and *A Novel Solution*

There's no mistaking excellent work, and Alex Pearl writes excellent stories. Novels that read like great films. Engaging, immersive, relatable. And funny. Leaving me sorry that *One Man Down* is now done, yet eager to read Pearl's next book.
Bill Arnott, bestselling author of the *Gone Viking* travelogues and *The Year of Living Danishly*

In *One Man Down*, Alex Pearl's biting satire on 80s individualism, London's adland is as much a character as Morse's Oxford. Run on two parts alcohol and one part cynicism, the sybaritic excesses of old Soho's creatives are the perfect accompaniment to this feast of theft, blackmail and murder.

Pete Langman, author of *Killing Beauties, Slender Threads, Black Box,* and *The Country House Cricketer*

A 1980s gem sizzling with witty dialogue and the mysterious murders of an advertising executive and a fraudster to boot. Alex Pearl writes from his personal experience of having worked in 'the glory days of British advertising.' Its tongue-in-cheek anecdotes and unashamed name-dropping of celebs like Julian Clary, had me laughing out loud. This is well written, entertaining, and different from the usual murder mystery.

M. J. Mallon, author of the *Curse Of Time* series: *Bloodstone* and *Golden Healer*

The worlds of cricket, advertising, and 1980s London can feel far away if you aren't British. But in Alex Pearl's capable hands they are made real — and very, very witty. Mr. Pearl clearly knows what he's writing about. The pace of the writing is brisk, but you'll want to take your time in order to savor the quips and puns. *One Man Down* is a highly enjoyable read!

Jadi Campbell, 2023 San Francisco Book Festival Winner with *The Trail Back Out*

This book is a great read for anyone who enjoys a nostalgic wallow in memories of the 1980s. The author evokes the detail of office life in the advertising business with pin-sharp precision. His protagonists, a lovable creative team, lead us through a world where real life events and cameo appearances by well known faces from the time give the reader a warm glow of recognition. Naturally, it's a world where murder is afoot and, whilst the main characters don't take on the detective role one might expect, they are nonetheless essential cogs in a tale that winds up with a satisfyingly unexpected conclusion. Lots of fun and highly recommended.

Review of *A Brand to Die For* by **Chris Chalmers**, author of six novels including *Five to One* and *Fenella's Fair Share*

The louche atmosphere and badinage of the 1980s is wonderfully conveyed by Pearl ... Anyone who wants a fast-paced read will enjoy this book with its unpredictable twists and turns, often darkly comic along the way.

Review of *A Brand to Die For* by **Eleanor Levy**, *Suburb News*

I so enjoyed reading this book. A glorious reminder of the advertising world in the pre-digital 1980s. Such happy memories of the attitudes we had — "below the line, beyond the pale" and so on. And the fun we had too. Alex Pearl's obvious enjoyment of language delights with playful plays on words and witty observations on human behaviour: "the bland leading the bland"; "Shakespearean copywriters getting bard-ons"; "cereal murderers doing porridge" and more. The engaging characters move the plot forward at a fast, easy pace.

Review of *A Brand to Die For* by **Hugh Salmon**, playwright (*Into Battle*)

Vividly written, and brought back many memories of what it was like to be in advertising in London in the '80s. I remember those watering holes well! Great fun and unfolds at a cracking pace.

Review of *A Brand to Die For* by **Peter Wise**, author of *Disturbing the Water*

A perfect book to take on holiday. Apart from a cracking plot, we're given a fascinating insight into the world of advertising. An added bonus — it's very funny!
Review of *A Brand to Die For* by **H. C. Denham**, author of *Almost Human*

I was asked by a young executive creative director recently, "Was it better in the old days?" Honestly, yes. This charming novel is evidence of it.
Review of *A Brand to Die For* by **Patrick Collister**, creative director and media commentator

Just like with *Line of Duty*, I love it when you start getting the back story to a character, then immediately think that they are a key part of the plot. Alex does this with pretty much every person in the book, leading you down several character dead ends and that was a great part of the tale. Just when you think you have cracked someone's role, something crops up to shatter that idea. I would love to know how Alex conducted some of his story research, particularly on aspects such as the terrorist cells, but it's probably best not to ask too much.
Review of *The Chair Man* by **Simon Pinell**, *Forward Magazine*

I don't think people with disabilities are well represented in the thriller genre, which *The Chair Man* goes a good way to addressing … I'd be giving too much away by going into detail, but this is a fast-paced revenge thriller with some fine action sequences.
Review of *The Chair Man* by **Chris Chalmers**, author of six novels including *Five to One, Light From Other Windows,* and *Fenella's Fair Share*

It is difficult to do this brilliant book justice in a short review. Anyone interested in reflections upon modern society and the impact of terror attacks, as well as those who simply enjoy a good book, will find this an engaging and involved read. The ending will also surprise them because it is certainly not anticipated.

Review of *The Chair Man* by **T. R. Robinson**, author of *Tears of Innocence*

Michael Hollinghurst is caught up in the 7/7 terrorist attacks in London. He survives but is left paralysed and in a wheelchair, but this doesn't stop him from seeking revenge against those responsible. And it's amazing what he can accomplish with a computer and a dog. The melding of real and fictional events is something I do in my books and I love seeing it in others. What really sells this story is the meticulous attention to detail, both in researching the facts of that fateful day and how terrorist cells operate, but Alex Pearl also goes into incredible detail when he's making stuff up, and that's why it can sometimes be hard to tell where fact ends and fiction begins, and I loved that! The short, sometimes very short, chapters keep the book moving along at a cracking pace without ever sacrificing detail, and much like reading Dan Brown, those short chapters constantly convince you that you always have time for one more. It's a great, original thriller with just a sprinkling of Le Carré, Tom Clancy and Ian Fleming's famous double-O.

Review of *The Chair Man* by **Philip Henry**, author of the *North Coast Bloodlines* series

More than a touch of John Le Carré in this. All aspects of it are incredibly well researched for a start — it truly feels like the author comes from the world of espionage and knows what he's talking about. The plot juggles multiple characters and storylines and moves along at a good rate. What I liked most probably isn't something that would immediately jump out to a reader, but: it's so English. Every time I picked it up again, I was whisked away to the UK ca. 2005/2006 and it was very

welcome. I haven't lived there for 10 years now, but it gave me a strong desire to go home.
Review of *The Chair Man* by **Grant Price**, author of *By the Feet of Men*, *Reality Testing* and *Pacific State*

Coupled with my fascination for the colloquial Londoner language, I was fully immersed into Michael Hollinghurst's world by the time the rising action went vertical. The tension grew to the point where I was nervous by the end, and the end was something I did not expect. *The Chair Man* by Alex Pearl is a well-researched and tense novel that I will not soon forget. I would say that Pearl has a new fan.
Review of *The Chair Man* by **Benjamin X. Wretlind**, author of multiple titles in the science fiction, dark fantasy, magic realism, and horror genres

Alex Pearl held me captive from page one. Powerful characters. An incredible plot that typically isn't anything I would read, but was so compelling I couldn't stop reading.
Review of *The Chair Man* by **Dawn Greenfield Ireland**, author of the bestselling *Hot Chocolate* series

A delightful fairy story that deals sensitively and compellingly with real, modern-day issues like homelessness, single mums and abusive parents.
Review of *Sleeping with the Blackbirds* by **George Layton**, actor, screenwriter and author of bestsellers *The Trick*, *The Swap* and *The Fib*

Its wonderful images and thought-provoking scenes moved me to tears.
Review of *Sleeping with the Blackbirds* by **Bramwell Tovey**, Grammy and Juno Award-winning composer, conductor and broadcaster

I devoured this wonderful middle-grade novel in less than 24 hours, and I loved it, though (or perhaps because) it turned out to be far more challenging than I originally thought it would be. Deeper. More profound. Touching on topics such as bullying, intellectual disabilities, illegitimacy, and parents in the prison system, it couldn't be more contemporary, yet it somehow has that old-fashioned feel so beloved by most fantasy readers.

Review of *Sleeping with the Blackbirds* by **Kelly Wittmann**, author of *An Authentic Experience*

Beautifully written, poignant and magical, Alex Pearl's writing style flows with the hand of a seasoned veteran. It pulls you in and never lets go.

Review of *Sleeping with the Blackbirds* by **Patrick Hodges**, author of *Jushua's Island* and *The Bax Mysteries*

I really loved this novel. I laughed out loud multiple times (which I rarely do while reading) and I was very moved at times as well.

Review of *Sleeping with the Blackbirds* by **Valerie Cotnoir**, author of *Your Home is Here*, *The War Within*, *Everlasting* and *Bridget's Journey*

The strength of the author's voice held me captivated long after turning the last page. With the wit of JK Rowling, Alex Pearl has definitely earned his place in the young adult fiction hall of fame.

Review of *Sleeping with the Blackbirds* by **Lisa McCombs**, Readers' Favorite

Alex Pearl has written a tale that is heartening and funny with the appeal of a Twain-like children's adventure.
Review of *Sleeping with the Blackbirds* by **Len Baker**, Suburb News

Alex Pearl deserves great credit for this excellent book. He has spoken to a hundred authors to delve into their working methods. It's very striking that he listens carefully to this wide range of people and allows them to open up as to what makes them tick as writers. The interviews are very interesting — not too long as to be daunting but long enough to learn a lot about each of the authors who took part in the project. It's obvious that Alex was able to make them feel relaxed and listened to and as a consequence they convey fascinating personal insights into the craft of writing. The range is vast from well-known writers to up-and-coming authors. Overall, a great project!
Review of *100 Ways to Write a Book* by **John Traynor**, author of the *Mastering Modern History* series

I was really chuffed to be asked to contribute to this fantastic project, and I wish I'd had this book on my bookshelf not just when I was starting out as a writer but throughout my career. There is so much wisdom here, I'd consider it an essential for new and established writers alike. I also love dipping into it and being surprised by how authors reveal themselves in their conversation with Alex. The variety of tips on how authors market their books alone is worth the book's (considerable!) weight. This is a terrific companion for everyone who writes. The fact that any proceeds from the book will be donated to Pen International (an incredible organisation that does fantastic work globally for writers in dreadful regimes) is commendable.
Review of *100 Ways to Write a Book* by **C. J. Carver**, author of 16 acclaimed novels and winner of the Crime Writers' Association Debut Dagger

One Man Down

Also by the Author

Sleeping with the Blackbirds
ISBN 978 - 1517130244

The Chair Man
ISBN 978 - 1675134948

A Brand to Die For
ISBN 979 - 8831526905

100 Ways to Write a Book
ISBN 979 - 8777608314

One Man Down

Alex Pearl

ROUNDFIRE
BOOKS

London, UK
Washington, DC, USA

CollectiveInk

First published by Roundfire Books, 2025
Roundfire Books is an imprint of Collective Ink Ltd.,
Unit 11, Shepperton House, 89 Shepperton Road, London, N1 3DF
office@collectiveinkbooks.com
www.collectiveinkbooks.com
www.roundfire-books.com

For distributor details and how to order please visit the 'Ordering' section on our website.

ISBN: 9781803417172
9781803417370 (ebook)
Library of Congress Control Number: 2023950541

A CIP catalogue record for this book is available from the British Library.

Design: Lapiz Digital Services

UK: Printed and bound by CPI Group (UK) Ltd, Croydon, CR0 4YY
Printed in North America by CPI GPS partners

We operate a distinctive and ethical publishing philosophy in all areas of our business, from our global network of authors to production and worldwide distribution.

One Man Down

For Colin, Ken, Tony, John, Shena, Chris, Paul, Mike, Pete, Hugo, Tony, Hugh, Robert, Penny, Toby, Borel, Martin, Silas, Alastair, Adam, Matthew, Caroline, Christine, Nicola, Cathy, Chris, Arthur, Roddy, Kevin, Carl, Linda, Sharon, Lucian, Mark, Stephen, Surrey, Ian, Graham, Jon, Snowy, James, Jenny and all those people I was fortunate enough to work with during the glory days of British advertising. This one's for you.

There are things that have to be done and you do them and you never talk about them. You don't try to justify them. They can't be justified. You just do them.

Mario Puzo, *The Godfather*

Preface

Following on from *A Brand to Die For*, this is my second in the Lovejoy and Finkle murder mystery series and is a kind of love letter to what was arguably the golden age of British advertising, which spanned the pre-digital era. This was the age of the eye-watering production budget and the infamous creative lunch that turned into supper and subsequently breakfast. As an advertising copywriter straight out of art college, I witnessed the burgeoning of this creative industry in London, from the sharp end, throughout the 1980s. Many of the locations that appear are real, and some of the TV advertising ideas, including the white lily being sprayed with perfume and colouring for Simple Soap, did in fact run on Channel 4. The Solid Fuel Advisory Service was a real client for whom award-winning work was also produced. And the idea for the Psion Organiser, the hand-held computer, was actually produced as an animatic with Roy Plomley's voice, but never made it onto our TV screens. The book will hopefully resonate with those who worked in the industry during the 1980s as well as enlightening those who didn't.

Although little research went into the writing of the book, I did need to visit the Hurlingham Club in order to gain a feel for the place and ensure that the details were accurate. And I'm indebted to Philippa Baldwin for showing me around both the club and the grounds including the cricket ground. I'm also very grateful to David Pearl, Hugh Salmon and Pete Langman who were good enough to read my first draft and suggest embellishments to the narrative. My thanks also go to Julian Clary for reading and giving his blessing to the passages in which he appears. And finally, and perhaps most importantly, my gratitude goes to the editorial team at Roundfire Books for their attention to detail, unwavering support and faith in the book without which it may never have made it onto the shelves.

Alex Pearl

Prologue

He was a portly, balding man of few words, and Angus could tell that he was going to be hard work. Bernard smiled at the client. "Let me introduce you to Angus Lovejoy and his partner Brian Finkle. These two reprobates created our award-winning real fires campaign."

Angus and Brian stepped forward and shook the limp, pudgy hand of the client who still hadn't said a word.

"Well, chaps, I think we may as well cut to the chase and reveal our proposed campaign to Gary here. Angus, would you like to do the honours?"

Angus was going to present but had suddenly felt terribly anxious, and he knew instinctively that Brian would be better with this guy. Brian would never get fazed by anything or anyone. He gestured to Brian who picked up the cue immediately. That's what Angus so liked about Brian. He always knew the score. They may have been very different in so many ways, but when it came to work, they were perfectly in tune with each other and on the same wavelength. It was undoubtedly the key reason for their astonishing success in such a relatively short period of time. There couldn't have been many, if any, creative teams in the business who'd gone and won a D&AD Silver for their very first TV campaign.

Brian pulled several presentation boards from a portfolio and placed them face down on the boardroom table.

"Let me, first of all, thank you for this opportunity to work on your brand. It's the first time Angus and I have had the pleasure of working on diarrhoea tablets ... And we can see this campaign of ours running and running ... To kick off, I'm going to present you our strapline for the campaign. As you know, your product is purchased predominantly by holidaymakers. So we have built our campaign around this premise and propose to run this strapline on all work that we produce — whether it be in print, TV or radio." Brian revealed the first board with a white headline reversed out of a black background. It read: *Don't let your stomach upset your holiday.*

Bernard chuckled to himself while the client sat stony-faced and totally unresponsive. Brian continued in his assured manner. "I'd like to show you our press concepts first," he said and then revealed a double-page spread that was taken up primarily with images of toilets. Underneath each was a location such as The Empire State Building, New York; The Uffizi Gallery, Florence; La Scala, Milan, and so on.

"As you can see," continued Brian, "we have here a veritable smorgasbord of public conveniences around the globe, and our headline reads *Tourist spots to avoid this summer.*"

At this point, the client scowled and chose to speak. "There seems to be a careless error in your layout."

"I beg your pardon?"

"Yes, a careless error. Third toilet from the right, bottom row ... It's all skew-whiff. Like I said, a careless error."

Brian laughed. "Oh no. That's not an error. It is deliberate ... You have to read the title beneath it."

Gary placed reading glasses on his nose and peered at the offending toilet. "Leaning Tower of Pisa ... I suppose you think that's funny."

Bernard was having none of this. "Well, yes. It's a bloody good joke don't you think? I peed myself when I saw that."

"Perhaps we should have titled it Tower of Pisser then," chipped in Angus.

The client scowled again. It seemed to be his favourite expression. "But there is no toilet in the Leaning Tower of Pisa. I know that for a fact. I have been up it."

"Well, obviously, there's no toilet," replied Bernard. "It was built in 1173. They didn't have them back then ... It's a joke."

"Doesn't work though, does it? The joke doesn't work ..."

Angus had had enough of this. "No ... I think Gary has a point. The joke doesn't work. Because as everyone knows, a good joke has to obey the laws of logic. Take any comedy that isn't logical and you can see that it isn't funny. Stands to reason. Look at Monty Python for example. Totally fucking illogical and bonkers, and as we all know, totally unfunny ... Or Spike Milligan and The Goons, which we all know is illogical and very, very unfunny. None of the millions of people who tuned into it found it funny. So on this basis, let me show you a whole bunch of other illogical unfunny ideas ... Here's a TV commercial you won't find in the least bit funny..."

Angus took a board from Brian's stack and held up a keyframe of the Statue of Liberty. "Now, imagine if you will, her arm being lowered and the sound effect of a toilet flushing." He picked up another board showing St Basil's onion domes in Moscow. "Now imagine the onion domes spinning around and the sound effect of a flushing toilet." He threw the board onto the table and showed another one of the Taj Mahal. "And now imagine the illogicality of the water level dropping as we hear the sound effect of a flushing WC ... Our final shot is of a plane in flight and as it passes us we hear the sound of a flushing toilet and our strapline appears on screen — *Don't let your stomach upset your holiday* ... I think we can all agree that this is totally illogical and therefore unfunny."

There was an awkward silence. Angus was seething. Bernard picked up the coffee pot that Nicola had placed on the table prior to the meeting and offered the client a cup.

"I think you miss the point, gentlemen." The client sipped at his coffee. "Whether or not this is funny is immaterial. The work you have shown me is flippant. It isn't serious. And it won't be taken seriously ... We are trying to sell a serious remedy to a serious health problem ... Diarrhoea is not trivial, and it certainly isn't a laughing matter. I think you have failed to grasp the brief, and I don't think I need waste any more of my time. Thank you for coffee. I shall see myself out." And with that, he was out of the door.

Angus thumped the table with his fist. "Arrogant and ungrateful little shit ... I need a pint. Who's going to join me?"

Bernard fumbled for his wallet. "I think we could all do with a drink after that. This one's on me, boys." As the senior account manager on the Solid Fuel Advisory Service account, Bernard had formed a close bond with Angus and Brian. Besides genuinely liking them, he knew only too well that his success was entwined with theirs. Having received universal acclaim for their witty TV campaign for real coal fires, the young team had not only won the agency awards and plaudits but also helped the agency lure new business and attract a host of blue-chip business prospects. On a more personal level, Bernard also had an affinity with Angus as both men were the offspring of remarkably small-minded and bigoted parents who had, to all intents and purposes, disowned their sons. In Bernard's case, for being gay, and in Angus's for being unconventional, or as Angus would put it, less up his own arsehole than they were. The two would often go to the pub together after work and bemoan the callousness of both sets of parents. For all these reasons, Bernard felt like a protective father figure to the young creative team and wouldn't think twice about fighting their corner.

Chapter 1

Angus lit his first cigarette of the day as they stepped out onto Great Pulteney Street and headed for their spiritual home, The Sun and Thirteen Cantons — otherwise known by one and all as The Tampons. "Quite appropriate, don't you think, Bernard?"

"Come again, Commander."

"Quite appropriate that we should have been shat on from on high by the Diocalm client."

"Oh, I see what you mean ..."

The conversation was very suddenly interrupted by a loud car horn emanating from a dark green Bentley with darkly tinted windows. All three of them looked in the direction of the car as the window on the driver's side was wound down and a bespectacled face sporting a distinctive ginger moustache popped its head out. "I say ... It's Shaggers, isn't it?"

Angus crossed the road and was followed by Brian and Bernard.

"Bloody hell ... Am I right in thinking that I'm talking to Bum Face?"

"You are indeed."

The two laughed heartily and Angus turned to Bernard and Brian. "Sorry chaps. Allow me to introduce you. This is Roy ... Roy Pickering who was at school with me ... What are you up to these days, Roy?"

"I'm a barrister by trade over at the Inner Temple ... Bit of a hobby to be honest ... Keeps the brain ticking over ... How about you?"

"Oh, I'm in the ad game for my sins and this is Brian and Bernard who I work with."

"Very nice to meet you chaps ... Bit of a long shot, but I don't suppose any of you chaps fancy a cricket match, only we're due to play at 1.30 at the Hurlingham Club but three of our players

1

have gone down with a dicky tummy … If memory serves, I do recall you being a rather nifty spin bowler, Angus."

"Yeah, I've been known to turn my arm over."

"Pretty good at getting his leg over, too," added Brian.

Roy laughed. "Talking of which, have you heard the news about the Chancellor's daughter, Angus?"

"Is that the same Chancellor's daughter who Angus got to know in the biblical sense in the school cricket pavilion?" enquired Brian.

"The very same lady," replied Roy. "Well, her engagement to Richard Emmery was announced today in *The Times*. Emmery by the way is a very eminent QC who practises from the set of chambers next door to ours. Small world, isn't it?"

Angus blushed. "Isn't it just?"

"Anyway, I digress from the matter at hand. What do you say to a game of cricket, gentlemen?"

"Thing is, Roy, we should be getting back to the office …"

"I wouldn't be so hasty, Angus." Bernard put his arm on Angus's shoulder. "Might be good for you and Brian to take the afternoon off. I'll clear it with Magnus. Don't you worry."

Angus paused and then looked at Brian. "What do you reckon, Brian?"

"I wouldn't say no … Funnily enough, I used to open the batting for my school."

"Well, that clinches it," added Roy. "Why don't you chaps slide onto the back seat?"

Angus took a final drag on his cigarette. "Tell you what, Roy. Brian and I will step up to the plate on one condition."

Roy looked at Angus apprehensively. "Alright, Shaggers. Name your price."

"We'll only play ball if you let us buy you a pint first."

***

The pub was unusually busy for a Monday afternoon. It soon became apparent why when Brian recognised another art director who worked next door at RHB. Apparently, they had just won a large piece of business from the government's Central Office of Information, and pretty much everyone in the pub was from the agency.

"Hi, lads. Good to see you. How's tricks? All drinks are on us by the way." The cheerful countenance now addressing them was that of Tom Haggard, the creative director of RHB.

"Hi, Tom. Not one of our finest hours, I'm afraid." Bernard offered Tom a cigarette.

"Oh, sorry to hear that mate. Client problems?"

"Prospective client … We just presented to a Gary Dixon …"

"Oh. Say no more. I've heard all about him. He was the marketing director at that new telecommunications company Orange for two minutes. Until he got found out. I have it on good authority that the guy is a prize dick. Where is he now?"

"Diocalm."

"Oh, nice."

"Problem was he had a bit of an accident in our office — all over the work."

"Nasty … Was it the boys' work?"

"Yep … It was a lovely campaign, Tom."

"Well, it would be coming from those two. Their real fires campaign for solid fuel is still the best bloody thing on the box." Tom looked at Bernard and then whispered in his ear. "You've done well to keep hold of them."

Bernard smiled. Tom wasn't wrong. Most teams that won awards would jump ship for more money, but Angus and Brian had felt some kind of loyalty to Magnus. And Magnus had managed to hike their salary pretty considerably.

"So, what's this piece of business you've pulled in?"

"It's the anti-smoking campaign. We were up against four other agencies. But they liked our campaign the most, which is gratifying."

Tom was a wily old fox. Bernard had heard on the grapevine that he had enhanced his already glowing creative reputation through a very clever deception. Apparently, he would brief several creative teams when pitching for business and give them at least four weeks to come up with campaign ideas. Then he'd sift through all the work and select the very best one and draw it up very badly on the back of an old envelope, which he'd then crumple up. This done, he'd phone the client and suggest taking them for lunch prior to the pitch. At the very end of the lunch, which would invariably be at his favourite restaurant, The Ivy, he'd pull the battered old envelope from his pocket and nonchalantly share the idea he'd had on the way to the restaurant. It was a brilliant ploy that never failed to impress and invariably won the agency the business on the basis that the creative director was some kind of creative genius.

Bernard looked at his watch and downed his free tomato juice. He was on the wagon and had given up smoking as part of his new fitness regime. "I'm afraid I'm going to love you and leave you, Tom. See you around."

Tom smiled. "Likewise ... And tell that creative director of yours to give me a bell when he has a moment. He owes me lunch."

Bernard turned to Angus who was in conversation with a couple of creative-looking long-haired blokes in leather jackets. "I'm off now, Commander. Some of us have work to do. I look forward to hearing a full match report in the morning." Angus downed the remains of the beer in his glass and waved at Bernard as he slid his way through the sea of bodies towards the entrance. At the same time, Roy stretched across and pointed to his wristwatch in an exaggerated fashion.

"Very nice Rolex, Roy."

"Good to see that you haven't lost your sense of humour, Shaggers … We'd better get on the road. Traffic will no doubt be crap, so we need to give ourselves ample time. And you'll both be needing some whites that fit." With that, the three of them followed Bernard out the door.

As they emerged into daylight, Roy spotted a traffic warden approaching his car and sprinted across the road. "Officer. We are about to leave. If you were kind enough to refrain from issuing a ticket, I will remain eternally grateful."

The traffic warden looked unimpressed and was about to speak when Roy continued.

"In fact, I'd like to go a little further in showing my gratitude by signing for you my latest novel." He opened the car door and stretched into the glove compartment and produced a pristine paperback carrying the image of an apple and the title *The Cider House Rules*. He then opened the book at the fly page and rested it on the bonnet of the car while signing J. Irving in a big flourish. "There you are." He handed the book to the somewhat bewildered traffic warden, climbed into the driver's seat and started the engine. All three of them waved gaily as the car slid away. The traffic warden flipped through the book. The back page was taken up with a large black and white photograph of the author John Irving staring back at him. He bore little resemblance to the man who had just handed him the book. It was the first time anyone had managed to get away without a fine, and he felt cheated. He raised his fist in the air and shouted one word to the departing Bentley.

"Wanker!"

***

Angus had never been invited to the Hurlingham Club before. He hadn't even heard of the place until now. Apparently, it had been around since 1869, and Roy had been a member since he was 18, as had his father. Roy parked the car quite badly at a jaunty angle to the kerb on Ranelagh Gardens — a smart terrace of red brick homes that oozed money.

Angus and Brian spilt out of the Bentley and followed Roy to the main gate, which was manned by an elderly gentleman with a walkie-talkie that crackled incessantly and a lanyard around his neck that carried a sombre-looking portrait of its owner who was a great deal chirpier in the flesh. "Hello there, Mr Pickering. Long time no see. How's life treating you?"

"Oh, we mustn't grumble, Eric. And how are you doing? I was so sorry to hear about the mishap on your bike. I take it you are fully recovered now and that the club gave you a reasonable period of paid leave ..."

"Oh yes. Thank you. They were marvellous. They even sent me flowers at the hospital."

"I'd expect nothing less ... You have been a dedicated and loyal employee for more years than I can remember ... Anyway, you take care of yourself, Eric. Lovely seeing you."

"Thank you, Mr Pickering. I do hope you have a good match today ... Lovely day for it."

The three of them carried on walking along a path that led past several manicured lawn tennis courts and over a pretty footbridge and equally attractive lake replete with ducks. The path continued through herbaceous borders and an impressive water fountain before snaking around the majestic old clubhouse that gleamed white as snow in the afternoon sunshine. The pavilion wasn't really a pavilion at all. It sat next to a magnificent old scoreboard with its own clock and was more of a marquee than anything else, being decked out in chirpy blue striped canvas with a veranda of sorts on which stood a couple of tables and deckchairs. The perimeter of the ground was punctuated with an assortment of handsome trees including an ancient yew, and close to the boundary a peacock was strutting majestically as if it owned the place. It was a lot prettier than the ground at Charterhouse, thought Angus. But he had fond memories of the place for entirely different reasons ... Extraordinary that the Chancellor's daughter had now bagged herself an eminent QC. Good for her, he thought, as they entered the canvas covered structure.

"Alright, chaps. Why don't you plonk yourselves here while I go in search of Alistair? ... I'll need your inside leg measurements."

"I'm a 29," replied Brian.

Angus looked a bit bewildered. "Sam buys my trousers ... I'm afraid I haven't the foggiest what size I am."

"That's alright ... Just whip your kellies off and have a look at the label ... It's perfectly alright, this is a changing room."

"Sure ... No probs." Angus removed his trousers and sat on the bench in his underpants looking for the label. "Ah, here we go. It's a bit faded but looks to me like a 32. I'll just confer with my art director ... What do you reckon, Brian? Is that a two?"

"Yep. That's a two alright. 32 is the correct answer."

And with that, Roy disappeared.

As a dressing room, it was basic but had everything they needed including benches, clothes hooks and rudimentary showers. And in the far corner of the changing room was a table on top of which sat an enormous leather cricket bag bulging with an assortment of new-looking cricket equipment. Presiding over everything was a large framed portrait of Her Majesty the Queen.

Brian removed his jacket and hung it on one of the hooks. "Beats the Ponders End local authority changing room block with its interesting graffiti that our school used to use back in the day."

Angus smiled. "Nothing like a bit of witty graffiti ... Gives a place some kind of soul, don't you think?"

"Not much wit in Ponders End, I'm afraid ... I think you'd have found it all rather depressing ... And the typos were pretty atrocious — even to an art director's eyes."

"Oh, Christ. That sounds like a nightmare ... There ought to be someone in charge of copy ... You know, making sure that four-letter words were spelt correctly by placing the c before k. And removing the apostrophes from unpossessive bastards."

Brian chuckled. "You should apply for the job."

"I already did. They turned me down. Didn't like my use of the Oxford comma."

There was a shuffling from the doorway as Roy returned with a pile of neatly folded cricket whites and chunky, cable-knit jumpers. "Here you go, chaps. These should fit the bill. You'll find a selection of cricket boots in the cupboard beneath Her Majesty."

"Ah, that explains it," remarked Angus.

"I beg your pardon, Shaggers?"

"I wondered why Her Majesty had that disapproving look on her face ... Must be that cheesy aroma of old cricket boots."

"Could be worse," added Brian. "Her portrait might have been next to the used jockstrap basket."

Roy pulled a face. "What a horrible idea. Thankfully, we don't have one of those."

As Angus and Brian began to undress, a wiry Sri Lankan with a neat goatee and smart little suitcase on wheels entered the changing room. Angus recognised him but couldn't quite place him. The Sri Lankan smiled broadly, exposing perfect pearly teeth. "My goodness. Shaggers! How the dickens are you?" As he spoke, Angus recognised the voice, and with the voice, came the name. It was Kumar Ranatunga, the class swot and mathematical genius who'd gone off to Trinity to study mathematics.

"Kumar. Terrific to see you. What are you up to these days?"

"It's a bit of a long story, but I'm now a builder in Margaret Thatcher's Britain ... It wasn't something I planned, but having studied mathematics and then architecture, I built my own house a couple of years ago, and now I've caught the bug so to speak ... By the way, have you heard about you know who?"

Angus gave him one of his quizzical looks.

"You know ... A certain lady you once knew ... intimately."

Angus blushed. "Oh, yes ... Roy filled me in."

"Her hubby-to-be is my client. I am building him, or rather them, a rather palatial abode in St John's Wood."

Angus raised his eyebrows. "What a small world it is ... Allow me to introduce my partner in crime, Brian Finkle."

Brian shook Kumar's hand. "Nice to meet you, Kumar. I have a great deal of respect for mathematicians. I'm not one myself, you understand. It was always a bit of a foreign language to me at school. But as my old man used to say, it was you guys who helped this tiny island stop Hitler from winning the war."

"Your father's not wrong. The role of mathematicians like Alan Turing has never really been fully acknowledged by the powers that be. He should be on every banknote. If we hadn't broken the Enigma code back then, who knows how things would have panned out? We might well now be living under the Third Reich."

Angus grimaced. "And we'd all be doing the silly walks — not just John Cleese. What a horrible thought."

As they spoke, another couple of players appeared at the doorway carting large holdalls. The larger and balder of the two introduced himself.

"Good afternoon, Roy ... With whom do we owe the pleasure?"

"This is Angus who was at school with me," replied Roy, "and this is his working partner, Brian. They are both advertising superstars."

Brian looked a little embarrassed. "I wouldn't go that far."

"Nonsense. Those real-fire commercials are among the best things on TV," added Roy.

"My goodness, are you behind those?" The balding man seemed genuinely moved and shook Brian and Angus's hands vigorously. "I'm Andrew Dunkley. I love those commercials with Brian Clough and Don Revie. They never fail to make me laugh."

"That's very kind of you, Andrew. And what line of work are you in?"

"I'm a struggling novelist."

"You are a proper artist, then ... What kind of stuff do you write?" asked Brian.

"I'm a crime writer and I write under the pseudonym Brendon Bolzwinick. But between you, me and the gatepost, it's bloody hard work for very little reward. Mind you, my agent is frankly bloody useless. And the publishers expect you to do all the frigging publicity. I sometimes wonder why I stick at it when I could probably do a lot better teaching English as a private tutor."

"What a great pen name. You can't give it all up with a name like that," said Angus, who was listening in on the conversation.

Andrew laughed. "It's Russian, and was my grandfather's name actually ... It is rather good, though, isn't it?"

"Bloody fantastic ... If I were you, Andrew, I'd hang in there. You've done really well to get an agent — even a crap one. I know how difficult it is to get one of those buggers. You must obviously be a talented writer. I'd love to read your stuff."

"Thanks, Angus. I'll get my agent to pull his finger out and send you a copy of my latest one ..." He produced a small notebook from his pocket and offered it to Angus. "Do you want to pop your address in here and I'll make sure my masterpiece wings its way to you in due course?"

As Angus wrote his address in the notebook, a constant stream of players arrived and parked themselves on the benches, and Roy, being the perfect host, introduced them all. There was Robin, the vicar; Alan, who looked pretty scruffy; Duncan, who was ludicrously tall and exceptionally smartly turned out; Barry, who was on the rotund side and was devouring the remains of a sausage roll; Jonathan, who was wiry and had an uncomfortably firm handshake; Ian who was wearing an old tweed jacket that had seen better days with leather patches at the elbows, looked like your typical academic; and Clifford, who was the only one already in his whites and was struggling with what looked like an oversized violin case.

"That's a funny-looking cricket bag you have there," remarked Angus.

Clifford smiled. "Actually, you're not entirely mistaken ... My cricket box is inside ... alongside my double bass."

Angus chuckled. "Of course it is. A protector within a protector. One for your instrument and another for your organ."

Clifford laughed. "Yes, indeed. How very delicately put."

"I take it you play the double bass."

"No, not at all. I just schlep it along as a conversation starter ..." There was an awkward pause. And then Clifford burst into laughter ... "Sorry, I jest. Yes, I play with the London Symphony Orchestra."

Angus had fallen into that one having asked a fairly daft question to begin with. But he liked this guy's sense of mischief. He reminded him of himself. "So tell me, Clifford, will you be providing us with a little serenade during the tea break?"

"Alas no. I don't think anyone has written a serenade for solo double bass. When they do, I'll let you know and will happily oblige."

Angus was about to say something mildly amusing when Roy interrupted by standing on the bench and clapping his hands. As he did so, a familiar face showed itself at the door.

Angus and Brian couldn't believe it. It was none other than Gary bloody Dixon. What in God's name was that pillock doing here?

Roy looked directly at Gary and grinned. "Ah, it's Gary Dixon, I take it. I'm Roy Pickering. Very good to meet you." The two men shook hands.

"When you are ready, Gary, we can toss outside. I have a coin in my pocket." Before Gary could answer, Angus stepped forward.

"Hello, Gary. How very funny to see you here ... And I mean funny in the peculiar sense."

Gary looked at Angus and went a shade of red.

"Oh, splendid. You two already know each other ... Always nice when that happens," added Roy. Then he turned to Angus and whispered conspiratorially into his ear. "Bit of a problem, Shaggers ..."

Angus could tell that something was troubling Roy. "Anything I can assist with?"

Roy looked as if he was in discomfort and took Angus by the elbow, steering him out of the dressing room.

"It's bloody Benjamin Bartlett. He's our opening bat and he's usually a real brick. He's always here early. Likes to practise in the nets ... Trouble is he hasn't shown up. And it's just not like him. In fact, it's totally out of character. So if we win the toss, I'm going to put them in first to give him time to get here. But if he doesn't materialise, do you think your man Brian would be up for opening the batting?"

"To be perfectly honest, I had no idea he played, but if he opened for his school team, one assumes he knows which end of the cricket bat to hold. And being the kind of bloke he is, I reckon he may very well be a decent player ... He will no doubt tell you he's rusty and a bit crap, but that's Brian all over. He's a very modest man, Roy."

Roy bit his lip. "On that basis, I think I'm going to ask him. But first things first, I'd better go and toss the coin with this Gary character. What's he like by the way?"

"Gary? He'll be fine tossing the coin. The man's a born tosser."

***

As Angus tied up the laces on his cricket boots, Brian took a seat next to him.

"Do you think Magnus will mind us taking time off like this?"

"I shouldn't think so. I think he's more worried that we're going to bugger off altogether. Bernard has more or less said as much …"

Brian nodded. "Yes. I guess you're right."

"And anyway, Magnus doesn't care about where we are. All he cares about is that we come up with the goods on time. So don't worry about it. Bernard is on the case anyway."

"Yeah. I'm sure you're right."

Angus gave him a cheeky smile. "By the way, a little bird tells me that you are going to be invited to open the batting."

"What?" Brian looked alarmed. "But I'm rusty and to be honest, a bit crap."

Angus laughed.

"What are you laughing at? It's not funny."

"Sorry, it's just the way you came out with it. You see, to me, Brian, you are unflappable and exude confidence like nobody else I know. But below the surface, it's all panic stations."

"Thanks a bunch."

"No, don't take it the wrong way. I mean it as a compliment. You are great under fire, Brian. This morning is a perfect example. There I was bottling it when that fat bastard sent out all the wrong body language and was clearly going to hate the work. And then you stepped up to the plate and presented perfectly — as cool as the proverbial cucumber. And I went and lost it altogether."

"You were right to lose it. He was never going to buy the work. And he was unbelievably rude. I think you pitched it perfectly."

"Thanks, Brian. But I'm not so convinced that shooting from the hip is necessarily the best answer." Deep down, Angus knew that this morning's outburst to the client had little to do with the fact that Gary Dixon was a charmless, uncreative client and everything to do with his parents showing scant regard for their younger son. He had received a rare telephone call from his mother only that morning to inform him that his older brother Julian was getting engaged and that he needed to put the date of their engagement party in his diary. Like his pompous father, she viewed him as a bitter disappointment. But then, he had been sent down from Charterhouse for shagging the Chancellor's daughter in the cricket pavilion, no less. And to add insult to injury, he'd then gone and sidestepped a career at the Foreign Office in exchange for one in advertising. The very thought of going into the unsavoury business of marketing would have given the Lovejoys palpitations. As a result, the telephone conversation had barely lasted a minute and not once did Mrs Lovejoy ask after her son's well-being or express any interest in his life. It was, in short, exceptionally hurtful, and had put Angus in an understandably and uncharacteristically bad mood that morning.

"Anyway, that's enough about me," continued Angus. "What I'm trying to say is that I'm sure you'll be fine at opening the batting. You always are fine, Brian. You just need to convince yourself. That's all."

***

It was a 1939 penny that had survived the war but George VI's youthful profile was looking the worse for wear, and it momentarily spun in the air and then came down to earth bouncing on the hard, dry turf. The two men knelt and peered at the worn piece of copper.

"Hard luck, Gary. Heads it is — in which case I will elect to bowl."

Gary looked a little surprised. Perhaps this posh geezer knew something he didn't. He'd never played on this ground before. He was used to fairly ropey wickets, some of which were on Greater London Council grounds. But their new fixtures manager was keen to up the club's game and had now arranged a spate of matches against clubs that had their own well-maintained grounds both inside and outside the M25, including several of the Oxford and Cambridge colleges.

"That's fine by me, Roy. Looks like a lovely batting strip." It was pretty strange, he thought, that those two lousy advertising oiks should turn up on the opposing side. He should have known better than to waste his time with any of those jumped-up, poncy advertising firms. He shouldn't have listened to their new marketing director.

"Alright, everyone! Gather round." Roy stood by the portrait of Her Majesty. It seemed like the right place for a leader to address his troops before going into battle. "We won the toss and have elected to bowl … Oh, shit! I've just remembered something important. We're still one man down. I'm going to have to find someone sharpish … Just give me a mo … Don't go anywhere, will you? I'll be back shortly." With these words still hanging in the air, he rushed out of the dressing room.

"That's a bit odd," said Clifford. "I thought Ben was playing today. Said he was looking forward to the game when I saw him a few days ago. He must have other fish to fry."

All nine of them were kitted out in neatly ironed whites. And for the next few minutes, they all sat there twiddling their thumbs.

Chapter 2

"Oh, bollocks!"

"What's up, Mr Cheerful?" Penny placed his black coffee by his typewriter, and Magnus looked up. For a split second, he considered telling Penny the truth. But no, he couldn't. It wouldn't be fair on her or on his wife Rebecca for that matter. They hadn't told anyone that they were expecting a third child. And he certainly wasn't going to tell anyone the latest results from the clinic. Results that suggested a 60/40 chance of Rebecca giving birth to a child with Down's Syndrome. They had shed buckets of tears over that piece of unexpected news, but they had both remained strong and resolute together and decided that they were going to have this child come what may. And they were going to support and love this child like any other.

"Sorry, Pen. Excuse my French ... It's just that I've seen this." He held up a single piece of A4. "It's a brief ... Not any ordinary brief."

"Bit of a brief brief, if I may say so."

"Very good, Pen. We'll make a copywriter of you yet. You're right though. It is a brief brief. They are usually the best. Bernard knows that and he's kept it really short and sweet. It's also the best brief this department has ever received."

"Well then, what's your problem?"

"My problem, Pen, is that I can't take it on because timings are tight and I have the sodding D&AD Awards to judge over the next couple of days — not to mention the creative brief for the Psion Organiser."

"I still don't get it. You have one of the best creative departments in town. One of your other teams will do something brilliant, I'm sure."

"Yeah … I know. That's the problem. I mean, it would have been nice to have had a go myself. It's been a while since I've picked up an award, Pen."

"You're the creative director. You get credit for your department's work."

"Yeah. I know. You're right. It's just my bloody ego rearing its ugly head."

"Will you give it to the boys?"

"What, Angus and Brian?"

"Yeah — the boys … That's what you always call them."

"I suppose I do … And it's a bloody good question." He took a sip of his coffee, lit a cigarette, and took a long drag. Then he rose from his chair and closed the office door and looked out of the window at the grey rooftops and roosting pigeons of Soho. "Thing is, Pen, I'm in a dilemma. If I give it to the boys, they're bound to come up with another award-winner …"

"But that's a good thing, isn't it?"

"Yes … and no. You see if they win another clutch of awards, it will be very difficult to keep hold of them … Bernard reckons that wily old fox Tom Haggard down the road has his eye on them, and he's probably right. They've just gone and won the bloody anti-smoking campaign. They are doing a lot better than us financially. They can probably afford to entice them with an obscene salary … I've already persuaded Ken to increase their remuneration significantly this year. I don't think we'd be able to match some counteroffer from someone like Tom. I'd be losing them, Pen. And I really don't want to."

"I know, Magnus. But I'm not so sure that they'll jump ship so quickly. They are comfortable here, Magnus. And they get a ton of support from you and Bernard — and they are given the kind of opportunities that they may not get anywhere else."

"So, tell me, Pen, what would you do if you were in my shoes?"

Penny laughed. "I'll need to sit in your chair and feel the vibes."

Magnus rose and gestured to his swivel chair. "Be my guest."

Penny sat in his chair and assumed the creative position with her feet on his desk. She closed her eyes and smiled to herself. "I'd get them in here and tell them that you have this fabulous brief for which you have a pretty good idea yourself, but you want to hold fire and give them a chance to have a crack at the brief as well because you love their work, and you only want this agency to produce the best work. And make it crystal clear that they and only they will always receive the best briefs from you. Tell them that is a guarantee that they can rely on because as far as you are concerned, they are your dream team. Then take them for lunch at The Ivy and talk about the brief. By the way, what is the brief for?"

Magnus sat for a few moments deep in thought. He had a funny idea that Penny would be worth hearing out.

"I like your thinking, Pen. They feel pretty comfortable. So make them feel even more comfortable. Guarantee that they will always get a crack at the best briefs and sacrifice my own opportunities for theirs ... Even huge sums of money won't get them that over at Tom's place ... Oh, the brief? It's for Simple Soap ... You know, the brand that has no artificial colouring or perfume. That's the single-minded proposition. And it's been signed off by the client. It's a wonderful brief ... Thank you, Pen. I appreciate that. Can I have my chair back?... Oh, and can you get onto The Ivy and book a table for four next Monday?"

"Four?"

"Yeah, four ... You're coming, too."

Chapter 3

Roy had to find someone — anyone. He was going to nip into the club bar and see if there was anyone he could approach, but before heading inside, he'd spotted an old boy in a deck chair wearing white trousers and a white cable-knit jumper.

Roy punched the air. "Thank you, God! I appreciate this, mate." He sidled up to the occupied deckchair and coughed.

The old man looked up rather startled. He had an impressive white moustache and could have been a descendant of W. G. Grace. On his lap was a copy of *The Magus* by John Fowles.

"I'm terribly sorry to intrude like this, but I don't suppose I might interest you in a game of cricket. Only you look like someone who might enjoy that noble game."

"Frankly, I'd probably enjoy anything more than this bloody book. Have you read it?"

"Ah, *The Magus*, yes indeed. It is bilge, isn't it?"

"Bilge? That's being terribly unkind to bilge."

Roy laughed. He liked this old cove. "Yes, fair point. It certainly isn't one of Fowles's finest efforts. *The Collector* was, on the other hand, a terrific debut."

"I agree. It was the reason I bought this one. Should have saved my money. Anyway, I wouldn't say no to a game of cricket. But it's a long time since I last played. And to be honest, I'm a bit rusty."

"Splendid. You'll feel at home playing with us then. We're all terribly rusty."

"Only one thing for it then. You'll all need to spend some time in the bar afterwards."

"Will we?"

"Oh yes. We'll all need to get well-oiled."

Roy laughed again. This old boy was a gem. "By the way, my name is Roy, Roy Pickering."

"Very nice to make your acquaintance, Roy. I'm Reggie Albright. Why don't you lead the way?"

***

As Reggie Albright took up his position on the mid-wicket boundary, Angus rubbed his hands and crouched down at his allotted place at first slip and watched Gary Dixon prod at an imaginary bump in the wicket with his brand-new Gray-Nicolls bat and check with the umpire that he was taking guard in line with middle and leg stump. That done, he patted the ground with his bat in an exaggerated manner to mark the spot and surveyed the field placings.

Angus blew his nose deliberately to break his concentration as Clifford, the double-bass player, started on his long run-up. "I hope you have some of your Diocalm to hand, Gary."

"Why would I want that?"

"Because this lad is so quick, he might give you the shits."

The bowler flew to the crease and in an elegant flurry of arms and legs released the ball. Angus was right. It was a fast delivery of good length pitching in line with middle stump. But Gary read it well and came down the wicket and drove it in the air off the front foot elegantly between long off and long on. The fielders gave chase but were never going to stop it, and it sailed past the boundary for six.

Gary twiddled his bat, adjusted his cap and smiled smugly.

***

While the Simple Soap task was undeniably a lovely creative brief, the other creative challenge that was occupying Magnus's grey matter at present was also potentially quite exciting. He'd had the idea for the Psion Organiser while he'd been walking the dog on Hampstead Heath the previous evening and now he was briefing John Reece, the illustrator, to draw up a storyboard. The Psion Organiser claimed to be a powerful pocket-sized computer — quite possibly the world's first. Though legally, that was always going to be difficult to claim. It was, however, most definitely a pocket-sized computer and that particular form of words had been cleared by the Advertising Standards Authority.

The idea was simple enough. It featured a character trying to walk with an entire personal computer system in his trouser pockets. The commercial would require a specially made suit and a very funny actor. But they'd only start worrying about that once the client bought the idea. John would draw up the keyframes for a rough animation known in the trade as an animatic, which would have the voice and music tracks laid on top. Animatics were useful when presenting to clients who had very little imagination, and nice readings by familiar-sounding actors never failed to impress.

As John laid out his impressive range of Magic Markers on the desk, Magnus picked up his phone and called Cathy in TV production.

"Hi, Cath. It's Magnus. We have John drawing up the keyframes for Psion as we speak, and I'd like to get the voice recorded ASAP. The problem is I'm going to be out of the office for the next three days judging the D&AD Awards. I'd normally ask Brian to stand in for me but he's going to be too busy. Can I leave it with you and Bernard to sort out?"

"That's fine, Magnus, but I've just heard back from Bernard Cribbins's agent. Unfortunately, Bernard isn't available for a week. But I was wondering if you might consider Roy Plomley?"

"Ooh, there's a lovely thought, Cath. Why not? He has a wonderfully warm voice. Does he do commercials?"

"I've just spoken to his agent. It was her idea actually. Apparently, he hasn't done any but isn't averse to taking on commercial work."

"Perfect. Book him, Cath. And just get him to read the script in his normal broadcasting voice as if he were doing another *Desert Island Discs* interview."

"No problem. I'll get back to his agent now and book a session at Silk Sound in the next day or two."

"You're a star, Cath."

***

Gary Dixon was playing better than ever. He was seeing the ball early and anticipating every small movement in the air and off the wicket. He was now on 49 and it looked as if the opposition were bringing on a new bowler. Oh, excellent, he thought to himself as the captain handed the ball to that prize plonker, Angus. He'd show him. Until now he had been fairly restrained and played well-timed strokes. He hadn't opened his shoulders and shown any aggressive brute force. But perhaps now was the time to have a bit of fun.

Angus hopped and skipped to the crease and lobbed a slow over-pitched ball towards Gary who couldn't believe his luck. He raised his bat high for the first time and anchored himself on the back foot and took a mighty agricultural swipe. It was his first mistimed stroke and by far the most inelegant. The ball caught a thick top edge and went sailing into the sky in the direction of Reggie, who looked extremely nervous as the ball began its descent towards him on the deep mid-wicket boundary. All eyes were now on Reggie as he peered up at the heavens and his spectacles twinkled in the sunlight. Roy was tempted to shout something but bit his lip. He knew from experience that it would only make matters worse. The ball was becoming increasingly visible through Reggie's Polaroid lenses and couldn't have picked him out more accurately had it been a heat-seeking missile. He raised both hands and gritted his teeth. The ball sailed straight through his hands and lodged miraculously between his knees. Roy couldn't believe his eyes and instinctively started shouting. "Reggie, whatever you do, don't bloody move a muscle, mate. In fact, stop breathing altogether for a minute." He ran at full pelt towards Reggie and swiftly plucked the ball from between his knees and held it aloft.

"Howzat!"

The aged umpire chuckled to himself. "Well, I never ..." And up went the finger.

Gary Dixon was furious. How in God's name could he get himself out to such an atrocious delivery and in such a ludicrous manner? Caught by an octogenarian between the knees! It was a travesty. He bashed the ground in annoyance with his bat and stormed off the ground with a face like thunder. Angus ran over to him.

"Now, in my book, Gary, that's what I call bloody funny."

Gary scowled and continued into the changing room.

***

"Ah, Magnus. Thank you for joining us. I thought this would be a good opportunity to introduce you to Keith Millward and Ian Vickery." Magnus closed the door of the boardroom behind him and shook the hands of the two white-haired gentlemen.

"Lovely to meet you both, and thank you for such a single-minded creative brief."

Keith laughed. "We weren't sure if we were being too lazy by not supplying you chaps with more ammunition so to speak."

Bernard poured coffee and passed plates of biscuits around. "Generally speaking, we like our briefs to be short and sweet with a pithy and compelling proposition. Yours is a perfect example, and I have to say that the proposition is very timely."

"Thank you, Bernard. Keith and I thought so, too. Anyone might think we paid that chap to write that book. What's it called?"

"*E for Additives.*"

"Thank you, Magnus. My memory isn't what it was. Terrible bloody name if you ask me. But it's all over the media, which, of course, is marvellous as far as we are concerned. And to be honest, Magnus, we see this as our biggest opportunity to make a real noise in the market. So let me explain what I was just telling Bernard here. You see, this year we thought we'd cut back on all our traditional sales promotion stuff and pour everything we have into a TV campaign with these new Channel 4 Johnnies who seem to be doing alright. We've got a pretty good deal with the station and have about three times as many spots as we'd get on ITV for the same money."

"I assume," added Magnus, "that we are promoting the range of products and not just the soap."

Keith helped himself to another biscuit and dunked it in his coffee. "I think we just need to show the range at the end of the commercial. As you know, it's pretty small. Just the soap and a couple of conditioners and skin creams. We certainly don't want to talk about specific products. We just want a brand commercial that conveys our raison d'etre. And we've agreed that the line: *Not perfumed. Not coloured. Just kind,* that appears on all our packaging should be our strapline at the end of the commercial."

Magnus nodded. "That's what I thought. Perfect. Now, the team I had in mind for this brief will I'm sure come up with something memorable and effective. If they were here, I'd introduce you, but they're out for the afternoon."

Keith smiled. "Not to worry. We'll be back in a few days to see their idea."

"Of course. That's the other reason I'm giving them the brief. They're very reliable when it comes to quick turnarounds. While most teams in this place require a minimum of two weeks to come up with a decent TV script, Angus and Brian tend to produce quality work in no time at all."

"They sound like a real asset," chipped in Ian.

"We appreciate that," added Keith. "So you won't be writing a script yourself, Magnus?"

"No, as much as I'd like to, I'm out judging the D&AD Awards as of tomorrow. And I have a fairly full schedule. To be perfectly honest, I'm a bit upset that I don't have the time because it's a fabulous brief that's crying out for an award-winning piece of work. Not that awards are the be-all and end-all."

Keith helped himself to more coffee. "Oh, I don't know. Awards are good for the soul, Magnus. I received a fair number of them for singing when I was a nipper. And do you know, I still have them? And in this business, if people like your ad enough to give it a bloody gong, then it's likely to be liked by the great unwashed ... Excuse the pun."

It was refreshing to hear a client enthusing about awards. Most clients were more concerned with sales results and didn't necessarily connect the two. Keith may have been one of the most elderly of their clients, but he was certainly youthful in his outlook.

"I'm certainly not going to argue with that, Keith. I had no idea you sang."

"In my younger days. Don't sing much these days though. But I did have a decent baritone voice back then. The only other bugger who won more awards than me at Eton was a chap called John McLeod. Think he holds the record. He's the Laird of Skye now, you know? Lovely bloke. Decent cricketer, I seem to recall. I'm reliably informed that he plays cricket for a bunch of musicians when in London called the Poet's and Peasants'."

Ian looked at his watch and put his plate on Magnus's coffee table. "Keith, I think we're going to have to take our leave."

Keith got to his feet. "Oh, my word. Is that the time already? Well, gentlemen, we will have to love you and leave you. We have a lunch engagement at 1.00."

Bernard picked up the phone. "Let me order you a cab. Where are you heading?"

"La Poule au Pot in Ebury Street."

"Very nice ... Hello. This is Gordon Deedes Rutter. Can we have a car please for La Poule au Pot in Ebury Street?"

***

Angus skipped up to the wicket and delivered the perfect off-break that pitched well up to the batsman who made to play a forward defensive, but the ball sharply turned towards the leg stump, between the bat and pad and clipped the bail, which wobbled and fell to the grass.

They'd got them all out for 123, and Gary Dixon had been the highest scorer with 49. Angus had taken eight wickets for just 40 runs. Roy was the first to slap him on the back. "Well played, Shaggers. That was a masterclass in off-break bowling. So pleased I bumped into you and Brian. We'd love to have you both as regulars — if you're up for it, that is."

Angus smiled. "Thanks, Roy. I can't answer for Brian, but I could get used to this. And Sam my girlfriend is keen on the game. She'd love it here."

"Splendid. Talk to Barry Gardner. We call him Billy Bunter. He's the one who was demolishing that sausage roll earlier. He's got a thing about them. But then, his old man was the world's largest producer of sausage casings or linings or whatever the bloody things are called. Anyway, he's our fixtures, membership manager and all-round organiser. He'll let you have all the membership details. Now, follow me. We'll decamp to the clubhouse and take tea in the Harness Room."

Angus nodded and ambled into the main house, across a marble tiled hallway and through a door into an elegant room where two long trestle tables had been laid with white tablecloths, china, cutlery and an assortment of very tempting sandwiches, cakes, scones and jam. Brian was already seated and in conversation with Clifford the double-bass player and formidable fast bowler. Angus sat next to Robin the vicar who was already tucking into a ham sandwich. He turned and greeted Angus warmly.

"Well, I must say it's a very great privilege to have the man of the match sitting next to me. Very well played if I may say so."

"You may indeed. Though I think I was a bit lucky. I haven't played for some years."

"I've heard that one before. I'm afraid I've been playing regularly for years and I'm still as hopeless as I was on day one." He passed the plate of sandwiches. "Do have a few sandwiches before Billy Bunter polishes them off. I can heartily recommend the ham and pickle. My wife made the pickle."

Angus didn't need much encouragement and lightened the plate. "Am I right in thinking that you are a man of the cloth? I think I detected a dog collar earlier."

"Well spotted. I came straight here from officiating at a funeral."

"I'm sorry to hear that."

"Oh, don't be sorry. He was 103. It was a celebration of a life well lived. Talking of which, I heard a lovely joke the other day. Would you like to hear it?"

Angus almost choked on his sandwich. "Go on then." This was going to be interesting.

"This chap goes up to heaven and he's waiting at the pearly gates and is greeted by an angel who asks him, 'Would you like to have a look around heaven?' And the man says 'Yes. Thank you very much. I'd love to have a look around.' So the angel shows him in and there are people milling around. And the man says, 'Who are these people here?' And the angel says, 'Oh, these people are the Muslims. And a little further along, we have the Jewish people. And if you'd like to follow me down this way, we'll see the Hindus, the Anglicans, and the Baptists.' And the man is very impressed but notices a very tall wall. 'And tell me,' he says. 'Why is there this big wall?' 'Oh,' says the angel, 'behind that wall, we have the Catholics.' And the man is a little perplexed. 'Why do you have the Catholics behind a wall?' And at this point the angel looks embarrassed and tells the man to keep his voice down. 'They like to think,' he continues, 'that they are the only ones here.'"

This time Angus really did choke laughing. "That's very good — particularly coming from a man of God."

"Yes, it never fails to raise a snigger. Can I tell you one more?"

"How could I possibly resist?"

"A vicar is conducting a funeral service at the graveyard having drunk a little too much communion wine earlier. Standing there in a not-too-sober state, he delivers the immortal words: 'In the name of the Father, the Son, and into the hole he goes.'"

"I think you're in the wrong vocation. You should be a comedian."

"Well, in a funny kind of way, I suppose I already am a bit of a clown. I like to keep my congregants laughing, Angus. We all need to laugh, don't we? It's the perfect medicine don't you think?"

"I couldn't agree more."

"I often think that Jesus himself must have had a good sense of humour. After all, he was a nice Jewish boy, wasn't he? And as we all know, some of the best jokes are Jewish ones."

"My partner, Brian, can tell you a few of those."

"Oh, I'll have to collar him later."

At this point, Roy tapped on a china cup and stood on a chair. "Sorry to interrupt tea. But I just wanted to ask everyone here if they'd seen Ben at all. Only it's most out of character for him not to turn up without telling at least one of us in advance."

The general consensus was that Ben hadn't materialised. Roy had thought as much.

Ben was a successful commercial photographer going through a stressful divorce. He'd recently moved out of the family home and was now living at his studio on the King's Road. Had it been anyone else, Roy wouldn't have given the matter a second thought, but this was so unlike Ben. He loved turning out for the club. He was a dedicated and very good opening batsman. Roy felt uneasy. Something was up. He stepped off the chair and then left the Harness Room and sprinted over to the clubhouse bar where there was a payphone. He pulled out some coins from his trouser pocket and dialled Ben's studio. There was no answer. Without thinking, Roy put the phone down and sprinted back outside and back down the path to the main entrance. It only dawned on him when he finally reached the car that he was still wearing his cricket boots with metal studs. The clatter of the studs on tarmac hadn't even registered. It was too bad. He wasn't going to go back to the changing room now. He'd have to drive the sodding car in his boots. As an undistinguished batsman, it would be the most impressive piece of driving he'd demonstrate in those shoes. The thought amused him as he turned the ignition key and gently pressed on the accelerator.

The traffic was reasonably light and he eventually found a parking space on the corner of Jubilee Place just past the ornate facade of The Pheasantry bar and nightclub that had once been a haunt of the great and the good and was now no more than a pretentious hangout for unemployed rich kids.

He rang the bell to the entrance to the studio that sat between two overpriced boutiques. There was no response, and there was no sign of his metallic blue BMW. Neither were there any lights on as far as he could tell from the pavement. He stood there for a few moments biting his bottom lip. There was nothing more he could do for the time being at least.

Chapter 4

Alf had seen it all at this place. He'd served pints to everyone from paupers to princes. That was no exaggeration. It was only last year that Prince Charles and Diana had made a brief appearance with their retinue and camera crew. Then there were the media lot and familiar faces from the telly. That Dave Allen fella liked to hold court in the corner with a whisky and a fag. Nice man, he thought. No airs and graces and personable to boot. Then, of course, there were the tourists. They all wanted to see the historic Dog and Duck and taste that famous warm beer. As he wiped a glass, he contemplated his retirement. He only had another six months at this place. Having been here for so long, he'd miss it. He and the missus were going to sell up and move to a little bungalow in Broadstairs. As he placed the glass on the rack, the phone distracted him from his reverie.

"Hello. You're through to the Dog and Duck."

"Hi there, Alf. It's Ben here. How are you?"

"Oh, you know. Mustn't grumble. What can I do you for?"

"I don't suppose Chaz is there is he?"

"Yeah, he's here. Shall I put him on?"

"Thanks, Alf."

Alf caught the eye of the man in the leather jacket who sidled up to the bar. "It's Ben. He wants a word."

"Cheers, mate. Can you put it through to the office?"

Alf winked and Chaz slipped into a small back room off the kitchen and picked up the phone while closing the door. "Have you got the shots?"

"Look, I've got the shots you wanted. But you didn't say anything about this bloke being a man of the church."

"Didn't think it was relevant. Anyway, why should that bother you?"

"Come on, Chaz. It's not some ordinary bloke on the street. This is the Reverend Simon Granger. He's a bloody Minister — a man of the cloth."

"Well spotted, mate. Dr Simon Granger, I believe. I hope the pictures of him and that boy are nice and clear."

"Of course, they are. That's how I was able to identify him."

"What's your problem, then?"

"My problem is that you've been economical with the truth. This is much bigger than you let on. And I'm not happy. Not happy at all. So this is what I'm going to do. I'm getting the shots couriered to you today with negatives. But I'm keeping duplicate negatives here until you pay me another £10,000. You have 30 days to get that money into my bank account. Once it is, I will destroy all my negatives. But if that money doesn't show up in 30 days, I'm going to the police and I'm going to tell them everything."

"You're bluffing. Why would you do that? You'll be incriminating yourself."

"Unlike you, I don't have a criminal record. And let me remind you that I'm not the one who's doing the blackmailing. I reckon the police will go light on me … You have 30 days. £10,000."

Chaz was just about to swear at him. But the line went dead.

Chapter 5

By the time Roy had returned to the Hurlingham Club, the match had resumed. Brian had apparently been playing very solidly. He'd only scored eight runs but had assumed the role of the opening batsman with ease and had seen off the fast bowler. Despite this, they had lost three wickets and only had 38 runs on the scoreboard. As soon as Roy sank into a deckchair, Clifford, who was batting with Brian, was clean-bowled by a yorker for 15. They were now 38 for four.

"Shit! I'd better get padded up." Roy disappeared into the dressing room with the thought of Ben's mysterious disappearance temporarily erased from his brain.

Chapter 6

Keith removed a panatella from his jacket, opened the window of the cab and lit up. "You know, Ian. I have a feeling in my water ... And I'm not talking about bladder and prostate bollocks ..."

Ian smiled. They had worked together for almost 30 years. Keith had offered him the job when Ian had been down on his luck, and together they'd grown the Simple brand from nothing. Today it was stocked by all the large supermarkets and high street chemists. They had a lot to be proud of.

"I think we may have struck gold with this Magnus chap, Keith. He's what my dear old mum would have called 'a good egg'."

Keith blew a long and exaggerated plume of cigar smoke towards the open window. "I agree. I like the cut of his jib, Ian. I genuinely believe that we are on the cusp of something big here."

"Well, you've always set your sights on turning Simple into a household name."

"And you've always dreamed about taking early retirement."

They both chuckled as the cab drew into the side of the road.

The cabbie turned in his seat as he pulled on the handbrake. "Here we go, gents. La Pole Oh Pot. French, I take it. Looks very nice. Wouldn't mind taking my missus 'ere."

"Indeed, it is ... And will you promise me something?"

The cabbie looked a bit confused. "And what might that be?"

Keith removed five ten-pound notes from his wallet, folded them neatly, and then planted them firmly in the cabbie's top jacket pocket. "Will you promise to bring your good lady wife to this very restaurant and treat her royally?"

"But I can't accept that, mate."

Keith smiled. "Oh, I think you can … Go on … Treat her."

"That's extremely generous, Sir. I certainly will. Thank you very much indeed."

"The pleasure is all mine." There was a spring in Keith's step as he strode towards the restaurant and held the door open for his partner. "Age before beauty."

"Thanks a bunch."

Keith laughed like a drain and stubbed out the remains of the cigar on the pavement. This was going to be one of those terribly enjoyable and exceptionally long lunches. God, life was good.

*****

Angus ambled out to the wicket in what looked like a brand-new pair of leather pads. He'd also opted to wear the club cap with its rings of blue, green and amber. Clifford had told him that the club colours were symbolic of the sky, the grass and the beer.

As he reached the square, Brian beckoned him over for a mid-wicket conference. He would no doubt want to talk strategy. Brian would almost certainly be looking to keep the strike. They needed to score 15 runs to win in five overs with no wickets to spare — Angus being the last man in.

"Angus … Looks like I've lost a fly button. Would you mind keeping an eye open for it?"

"No problem, mate. Wouldn't want your todger to make an unexpected appearance."

And with that, they both stepped back to their respective ends and Brian took guard. The bowler turned, trundled in and delivered a medium-paced ball of good length and Brian clipped it deftly and rather elegantly between mid-wicket and square leg. They settled for two comfortable runs. The next two balls were dispatched by Brian to the deep square leg boundary.

And on the last ball of the over, he played a cheeky little dab off the back foot between second slip and gully for an easy single. He had kept the bowling and now only needed four runs to win from Gary, who had been brought on to bowl.

Gary took his overly long run-up and trundled in like an ungainly juggernaut in second gear. The ball was decent enough but Brian was now seeing it very well, came down the wicket and smacked it off the meat of the bat and it rocketed at waist height straight back to the bowler. Gary instinctively went for the catch but wasn't quick enough and was struck squarely in the nether regions. He doubled up in agony and lay prostrate in the middle of the square as Angus and Brian completed the first run. The ball had been struck with such force that it had been deflected to deep mid-wicket, and Brian had called Angus back for a second run. As he did so, the fielder picked up the ball and threw it as hard as he could. The ball miraculously flew towards Angus's end, bounced once and then demolished the middle stump before Angus could make up his ground. He'd been run out. It was all over.

Brian tucked his bat under his arm and apologised to Angus. "Sorry, mate. It was my fault. I shouldn't have called you back for that second run ..."

"What are you talking about, Brian? In my book, that was a bit of a result."

Brian looked a bit confused. "But we just lost."

"I don't think so. Just take a look over your shoulder, mate."

Brian glanced behind them. Gary was still lying on the ground with a couple of ground staff in attendance.

"See ... Now that's what you call a result. In fact, I think it might be time to bring on the new balls."

Chapter 7

Magnus grabbed a piece of toast from the toaster and smeared it with Marmite.

"I'm off now, luv. I'll see you later." He grabbed his bag and coat and opened the front door. It was a distinctly grey morning, so he took an umbrella from the cupboard.

The cabbie was sitting in his cab smoking while Magnus let himself onto the back seat.

Number 12 Carlton House Terrace was a distinctly posh location for any kind of convention, let alone one designated for a group of largely long-haired blokes in leather jackets and open-necked shirts. But then, this elegant Regency address that sat on the south side of Pall Mall, alongside St James's Park, was the home of British Design and Art Direction, the body set up in 1962 by a bunch of designers, art directors and photographers including the photographer David Bailey to promote excellence in advertising and design. The organisation was best known for its annual awards event and the publication of a lavish hardback annual in which winners' work was displayed and credited each year. The organisation had, in a relatively short space of time, established itself as one of the industry's most respected awards bodies in the world.

Magnus stepped out of the cab and trotted up the steps to the majestic columned portico. He felt flattered to have been asked to take part in judging, but the name of the organisation never failed to rankle with him. Why for fuck's sake had they confined its title to just bloody designers and art directors when everyone knew that it was the bloody copywriters who were, more often than not, the individuals who brought most to the party; namely ideas and words?

The room was full of serious-looking men grouped in huddles balancing cups on saucers and speaking in hushed tones. You could easily tell the copywriters from the art directors. The copywriters were generally less well art-directed, and slightly rough around the edges. Almost all of them wore t-shirts or open-necked shirts that had seen better days. Magnus's mother would almost certainly have described them as "unkempt". Some were even smoking. The art directors, on the other hand, were neat and tidy. Some sported shirts and ties while others wore expensive-looking knitwear. The designers were even more fastidious in tailored suits.

Magnus headed for the table at the far end of the room that was laden with china cups and saucers behind which a couple of young girls were serving tea and coffee. As he accepted a strong black coffee and lit his first cigarette of the day, he felt a tug at his elbow.

"Magnus. I had no idea you were taking part in this gig."

Mark Manners was another copywriter that Magnus knew from a previous life when they had been rivals at DMC&C. As far as looks were concerned, Mark didn't fit the classic copywriter mould. He always wore expensive designer labels, and unlike most copywriters, didn't possess much of a sense of humour. On one occasion Magnus and his then-art director had carefully removed a designer label from Mark's jacket that had been hanging in reception and replaced it with a Marks and Spencer label. A week later when Mark was leaving a restaurant in Soho and been handed his jacket by the cloakroom assistant, he spotted the offending label and immediately sent it back in the firm belief that the jacket could not have been his.

"Oh, hi there, Mark. How are you? It's been a while."

"Well, thanks. So, what are you judging?"

"Oh, Consumer Press, I believe."

"They've given you the big one then. They've put me on the bloody Direct Marketing panel. Still, I guess it's better than a poke in the eye with a sharp stick."

Magnus sipped at his coffee. "I don't know. I think I might have opted for the sharp stick." He couldn't resist the jibe. But then immediately felt a bit guilty. Mark may have been a pain in the neck but he wasn't a bad bloke. "Are you still working at FGN?"

"For my sins, yes. I nearly left last year but they offered me the role of Head of Copy and I'm now working with the lovely Ron Sanders." Sanders was an industry legend. A talented art director who had been in the business longer than anyone and had won more awards than Fanny Cradock had had hot dinners.

"Lucky old you. What's Ron like to work with?"

"He's brilliant before lunch, but after lunch, you can forget it."

Magnus had heard all the stories about Ron Sanders and his unfortunate drinking habits. An account man had apparently once discovered him after lunch out cold on a sofa in his office and declared, "Ron, call yourself an art director? You're in no fit state to draw anything — including a fucking salary."

***

In the far corner of the room a tall gaunt-looking man offered the portly man next to him a cigarette.

"Can I assume then that we have a deal?"

The portly man accepted the cigarette, lit up and took a long drag while keeping a beady eye on everyone else in the room. He expelled cigarette smoke towards the high vaulted ceiling with its delicate plasterwork and, without saying a word, discreetly nodded.

***

Magnus was running out of things to say to Mark and was beginning to wish that he hadn't been collared by him in the first place when he was tapped on the shoulder and turned to see a familiar-looking face.

"My goodness, what are you doing here, Magnus?"

It was the photographer Jeremy Mason who'd shot some ads for the agency a couple of years ago. If memory served Magnus correctly, it had been for that revolting lager Arctic Lite that

Allied Breweries were now flogging to diabetics on account of it being very low in sugar.

"I might ask you the same question, Jeremy."

"Oh, I'm here to judge the photography. And I was quite excited by the prospect of judging my own work, but apparently, we aren't allowed to do such a thing; more's the pity. I was rather looking forward to taking some of those cute pencil awards back to the studio."

Magnus smiled. "The official line is that nobody can vote for their agency's work, but there are ways and means, so I'm told. Allow me to introduce you to Mark Manners."

Mark grinned broadly. "Nice to meet you, Jeremy ... Actually, the first agency I ever worked at decided that it was about time they won some awards. Trouble was they were a crap agency and its creative director couldn't tell shit from sausages. So the agency came up with a very cunning plan. They designed their own awards scheme; called it the A Awards; had the accolades cast in silver-plated bronze; and then awarded themselves a whole bunch of the things. It was actually cheaper doing that than paying the entrance fees for submissions to genuine award competitions that they were never going to win. And I have to say, their display cabinet in reception looked very impressive."

Jeremy chuckled. "It's not such a dumb idea. Did the clients buy it?"

"I've no idea. I didn't hang around long enough to find out. But they weren't the kind of clients that would have cared two figs ... Talking of awards, have either of you discovered yet who else is judging on your panel?" Both Magnus and Jeremy shook their heads.

"The only person I know to be judging with me is Ben Bartlett," said Jeremy, "but the bugger hasn't shown up yet as far as I can tell ..."

Chapter 8

Amanda Huggins couldn't believe her luck. She hadn't gone to university. Instead, she'd done the travelling thing to get it out of her system. Four months of lemon-picking on a kibbutz in the Lower Galilee in northern Israel followed by another couple of months trekking around Greece and Turkey. Now she was back home living with her middle-class parents in their middle-class 30s detached pile in Esher, from where she had applied for the position of Parish Secretary at St Peter's Church, Hammersmith. As a very bright, vivacious and excellent typist with a speed of 120 words a minute, she had made quite an impression at the interview, and shouldn't have been so surprised at being offered the job. Her boss would be none other than the Reverend Dr Simon Granger. It was all terribly daunting at first. But she needn't have worried; Granger turned out to be utterly charming, and had put her at ease from day one. The fact that they both shared the same quirky sense of humour and affection for cats also helped matters.

Her office, though bare, was capacious. She had her own desk, filing cabinets, IBM electronic golfball typewriter, and telephone, which now sprang to life.

"Good morning. You are through to St Peter's Church. Can I help you?"

There was a pause at the other end, which was eventually broken by a slightly gruff South London accent of a man — the kind of man that Amanda would instinctively steer clear of.

"Yes. You can put me through to Reverend Granger."

"I'm afraid Reverend Granger is indisposed at the moment. Can I ask who's calling?"

There was another pause.

"My name is Chaz and I need to speak with Reverend Granger as a matter of urgency. As one of his congregants, I demand to speak to him now."

"Well, I can arrange an appointment for you to see him in person after Evensong tomorrow..."

"As I said, it's urgent. If I don't speak to him now, I will have to go to the newspapers. And to be honest, I don't think Reverend Granger would like that. Do you?"

Amanda didn't like the sound of this man one bit. He gave her the shivers. She was tempted to hang up on him. But deep down, she knew that he meant business and wasn't going to go away.

"Will you hold the line one moment, please?" She put the receiver on the desk and then made a transfer call to the vicarage.

"Good morning, Simon Granger here."

"Reverend Granger. It's Amanda. I'm sorry to interrupt your morning schedule, but I have a congregant on the phone called Chaz who insists on talking to you now."

"I can see him after Evensong tomorrow..."

"Yes, I know. I told him so. But he then became insistent and rather menacing and said that if you didn't speak to him now, he'd go to the newspapers."

"Are you alright, Amanda?"

"I suppose I'm a bit shaken. I didn't like the sound of him."

"Put him through. I won't tolerate these people being rude and unpleasant to you."

There was a click on the line as Amanda put the call through.

"Hello. This is Reverend Granger. Who am I speaking to?"

"Never you mind who you're speaking to. Thing is I know who you are. You, Reverend Granger, are a fraud. You are a raving homosexual who is cheating on your wife. Am I not right? And the bad news for you is that I can prove it. You see, Reverend Granger, I have photographic evidence of your sordid exploits. And should any of this photographic evidence come to light, your whole career and marriage will be over. Poof! Just like that. Appropriate word, poof, don't you think? You see, Reverend Granger, I have friends in the media. People at the *News of the World*, the *Daily Mirror*, the *Daily Mail*. They'd all give their eye-teeth for a story like this, Reverend Granger. They'd pay me a king's ransom for a story like this. But I'm a fair man, Reverend Granger. So I'm giving you the chance to save yourself."

"How much do you want?"

"£50,000."

"£50,000? You're mad. I don't have that kind of money."

"You have powerful friends, Reverend Granger. You can't tell me that you don't have ways and means to raise a loan through your wealthy colleagues in the church."

"It's not that easy."

"As I say, Reverend Granger, I can easily get paid by the media. I will call you back in three weeks. That's how long you have to get the money. But I warn you. If you go to the police, the photographs will be sent directly to the press. So no funny business, Reverend Granger."

"How do I know these photographs even exist? You could be making all this up."

"You will receive copies in the post tomorrow. Once I receive your payment, the negatives and all copies will be destroyed. Speak soon. Toodle pip."

The line went dead.

As Granger put the phone down, there was a tapping on his door.

"Come in."

A petite and not unattractive young woman in denim jeans and cashmere cardigan entered with a tray of tea and toast coated in marmalade.

"Here you go, darling." She put the tray down amid the papers and a redraft of Sunday's sermon. She kissed him on the forehead affectionately.

"Is everything alright? You look a bit like a hare caught in the headlights of an oncoming car."

He forced a laugh. "Sorry, darling. I'm miles away. I was thinking about Sunday's sermon."

Chapter 9

"For Christ's sake, Ben, will you stop shagging some piece of fluff and pick up that sodding phone."

Melissa Bartlett hadn't lost her good looks. Nor had she seen any of her clients fall by the wayside over her imminent divorce. She was a smart cookie and she knew it. At 42 she was still giving those young fillies a run for their money and was still getting plenty of work from some of the world's leading fashion houses. While Ben's work paid pretty well, it had always been fickle. Her work, on the other hand, had been consistently reliable, and her fees were becoming increasingly lofty despite her advancing years.

Now, of course, Ben had come to rely on her financially more than ever. And that was why she was calling him now. She'd lent him 20K before his next big job came in to tide him over. It was a lot of money for most people. But for Melissa, it was loose change. Besides earning well, she'd discovered the art of investing well and with the aid of her subscription to *Investors' Chronicle*, had become something of a dab hand when it came to company shares, unit trusts and investment trusts. And she was one of the few people to openly applaud Chancellor Nigel Lawson's plan to introduce tax-free investments. As far as she was concerned, it was a huge opportunity for people like her to shelter those canny investments from the reach of the tax man. She may have been financially astute and independent, but she wasn't overly extravagant with money. And nor was she going to write off the 20K loan to Ben. In this respect, she had principles. He had agreed to pay her back by the beginning of June and today was the 25th. She'd been more than fair. Now it was time for him to pay her back.

She didn't hate him, and as far as she could tell, he didn't hate her. They had just grown tired of each other. The divorce had been perfectly amicable. She had been the one who had instigated it, but everything had been civilised, if a little stressful. He'd agreed to move out of their substantial terraced Victorian pile that sat on a tree-lined road off the expensive and most desirable end of the King's Road and she had agreed to buy out his half at the prevailing market price.

She put the phone down with an air of resignation and rifled through a drawer for her Filofax. There was someone far more engaging and worthwhile to talk to and unlike her useless husband, he was certainly going to pick up.

***

Simon Asquith was pretty wet behind the ears. He'd been quite lucky to get this job. He had his Uncle Michael to thank for that. His mother's younger brother was senior clerk further down the road at number seven King's Bench Walk, and doing very nicely, thank you very much. So nicely, in fact, that he had recently moved his growing family to a spacious four-bed semi in the up-and-coming environs of Putney.

Simon may not have been an academic, which his dismal O-level results would attest to, but he was certainly nobody's fool. Indeed, he was a great deal sharper than most junior clerks. And he sensed that this particular phone call was of a very sensitive nature and would require privacy, which was in short supply in these chambers. He couched the receiver in his hand and glanced over to his boss's office. The glass door was closed and through the glass partition, Simon could make out Andrew smoking a cigar while in conversation with one of the barristers.

"Would you excuse me one moment?" He put the receiver down and strode over to the smoke-filled office and tapped lightly on the glass door.

"Is it urgent, Asquith?"

Simon nodded and turned the handle. "I'm sorry to intrude, Sir, but a rather sensitive and important phone call has just come through."

Andrew stubbed out his cigar and the other man rose from his seat. "Thanks for that, Andrew. I'll get onto Graham in the morning. I think his expertise will come in useful in the light of the new evidence." He brushed past Simon. "He's all yours."

As the door closed, Andrew gestured to the seat and Simon sat opposite his boss.

"How are you settling in, young Asquith?"

"Well, thank you, Sir."

"Good. I'm hearing good things about you on the grapevine. And that's something I rarely hear myself say to junior clerks. So keep it up and you'll be following in your uncle's footsteps … Now, what is this sensitive call all about?"

Simon looked tentatively through the glass at the other barristers.

"Oh, it's that sensitive is it? Well, you'd better come a bit closer and whisper in my ear."

Simon rose from his leather seat and approached his boss.

"I have a Chief Inspector Goldman on the phone, Sir. Says he wants to talk to Mr Pickering urgently about a personal matter that has nothing to do with Mr Pickering's work. Says he'd like to come over and talk to Mr Pickering in person."

Chapter 10

The headline on the front cover of *Campaign* magazine caught Angus's eye as he stubbed out his cigarette. *Award-winning photographer reported missing.* He continued reading.

As this publication goes to print, the Metropolitan Police have announced that the award-winning advertising photographer Benjamin Bartlett has gone missing in suspicious circumstances. His apparent disappearance had been reported by his estranged wife Melissa Bartlett, who had been attempting to speak to her husband for some days. Mrs Bartlett is in the process of divorcing her husband but is on good terms with him.

The case took an ominous twist earlier today when police discovered Mr Bartlett's abandoned metallic blue BMW at West Wittering along with a suicide note. Clothes were also found on the beach, which are believed to have been Mr Bartlett's.

Chief Inspector Goldman, who is heading up the enquiry, has told Campaign magazine that it is too early to speculate about the case. "Sadly, people go missing every week," commented Goldman. "And when suicide notes are found, we can't always assume the worst. In this instance, there is no body. While that remains the case, we will continue to keep an open mind."

Brian was flicking through a photographer's folio while the young female agent sat pensively with a mug of coffee on the sofa.

"Bry, have you read this story about that snapper Ben Bartlett?"

"Wasn't that the guy Magnus used for Long Life Beer?"

"It was indeed. Anyway, he's gone missing and the police have discovered his abandoned car and suicide note."

Brian looked up from the folio. "What? You're kidding."

"No. It's here in black and white. Front page of *Campaign*, no less."

"That's terrible. I wonder if Magnus knows."

"I think I smell a rat." Angus lit another cigarette and took a long drag. "I bet he had life assurance. Photographers are well-versed in the world of insurance. Most have their priceless equipment and stuff insured for squillions. You can bet your bottom dollar he also had life assurance."

"What are you suggesting?"

"Well, he's getting divorced, isn't he? And his wife may not be his best friend at present."

The girl on the sofa suddenly became quite animated. "I have a friend who shares the same cleaner as Melissa Bartlett. And she's apparently a bit tight with money despite being loaded."

Angus picked up the phone. "I have an idea ..." He tapped at the dials as Brian watched him intently. "Hello. Is that the operator? Can you put me through to the Soho Model Agency? ... Hello. Am I talking to the Soho Model Agency? Excellent. Would it be possible to leave a message for Melissa Bartlett? Could you tell her that Angus Manilow called? I'm her husband's financial adviser and I'm trying to track down her husband about his life assurance policy ... Could you pass on this telephone number please: 01-434 0040 extension 23? If she could call Angus at the earliest opportunity, please, that would be hugely appreciated. Thank you." He put the phone down. Two minutes later the phone rang back. "Hello, Mrs Bartlett. Thank you so much for calling back. My name is Angus Manilow. I'm trying to track down your husband. You see, he has a life assurance policy with us. Were you aware of that, Mrs Bartlett? You were ... Good ... Well, we recently had a conversation about reviewing his premiums ... Yes, that's right, his monthly payments to increase the lump sum pay-out in the unfortunate and unlikely event of his demise ... Well, I don't know Mrs Bartlett why he would want to raise the pay-out from its current level. But I'm sure Mr Bartlett had his reasons. I don't suppose you know where I can

find him? I'm having a terrible job trying to get hold of him ...
Oh, I see. Well, thank you, Mrs Bartlett. Good day.

"What did I tell you? The bugger is insured — probably to
the tune of squillions. She'd have every reason to want him to
pop his clogs."

Chapter 11

He hadn't been back to Margate for years. He'd seen his mum, of course. They'd had her to stay with them in Chelsea on numerous occasions. In fairness to Melissa, she'd been pretty bloody good about it. She'd lost her own mother to cancer when she was only 18, which was almost certainly the reason she didn't mind having her to stay. Now he felt ashamed that he hadn't been down for so long. The place was a complete hovel, and was, like much of Margate, falling apart at the seams. And she wasn't in much better shape herself being partly deaf and in the early stages of dementia. Mind you, he could talk. Look at him. His life was a complete bloody mess. He was in the process of getting divorced; was up to his ears in debt; work had more or less dried up; and he was beyond coping anymore. He couldn't bear the indignity of suffering another bloody handout from Melissa, but that said, doing a runner probably wasn't going to solve anything.

Come on, Ben, give yourself a break. You had to fuck off. For your own mental well-being. You know that better than anyone. You'd have completely lost it otherwise. You needed space. Space to bloody breathe …

"You alright, luv? … You've gone all quiet."

He opened his eyes and the faded and peeling wallpaper from his youth came back into focus. "Yeah, I'm fine, mum. Just thinking about the old days."

"The old days … We had it hard back then. But say what you will, I tell you one thing. We all pulled together in them days. We all mucked in. Didn't matter where you came from — which side of the tracks you came from, we was a united country. All pulling in the same direction. The king and the queen, that lovely queen, they stayed you know."

"Did they?"

"Course they did. They could have buggered off to Balmoral, away from the bombs. But they didn't. They chose to stay in London in the Blitz. They chose to sit it out with their people. That's what I call real patriotism — love of one's country and people. That was the old days. They may have been tough days, but them were good times, Ben."

Ben smiled and sipped at his instant coffee that had now gone cold. "Wish I was strong enough to face the music, mum."

"Don't talk to me about music. The stuff they play these days isn't music. Dad and I used to go to tea dances before the war. Benny Goodman and Glenn Miller. Now that's what you call music ..."

***

Andrew decided that it would be best if he excused himself from chambers for fifteen minutes. He didn't want to have to tell the others that Roy required his office to talk to a Chief Inspector about something personal. Simon was a bright lad. He'd done the right thing. As far as Andrew was concerned he'd sit here with *The Telegraph* and a strong black coffee he didn't really want and just sit it out. He looked at the newspaper's headline: *September baby for Princess Diana*. Apparently, she was expecting a second child. But it held little interest for him. Instead, his mind turned to Roy and this strange interview with the senior policeman. He was obviously intrigued and would love to have been a fly on the wall. He liked Roy a lot. He was polite and could be quite funny at times. And was a bloody good barrister. And unlike so many public school boys who passed through his chambers, there was no arrogance or conceitedness to the man. It was also apparent that Roy was almost certainly the most affluent member of chambers having inherited his father's vast fortune and family seat. But he didn't splash the cash. His only outward signs of wealth were his ancient Bentley, which he inherited from his father, and that cut-glass accent.

***

"I'm sorry to impose on you like this, Mr Pickering, but we are very concerned for the well-being of a Mr Benjamin Bartlett who I understand you know."

Roy removed a packet of Marlboro cigarettes from his jacket and offered one to the inspector who politely declined, before lighting one himself and taking a long drag.

"I knew something was up. I think it's me, Inspector, who probably needs to do the apologising. I should have called you myself. I had a feeling when he didn't show up for the cricket match on Thursday afternoon. Do you mind me asking how you got onto me, Inspector?"

"You were the last person to leave a message on his answer machine, Sir. And his wife, Melissa, filled in the rest."

"Yes, I did leave a garbled message. I went round to his flat during the tea interval. It wasn't like him, Inspector, not to turn up to a match without telling us in advance. But there was no sign of the bugger. I had a feeling something was seriously awry. Has his wife spoken to him recently?"

"No. She was due to meet him for lunch on Wednesday but he never showed up. I take it then that he's a keen cricketer?"

"They don't come much keener than Ben. He always shows up early and likes to have half an hour in the nets before the match. You see, he always opens the innings for us. He's a very reliable opening batsman. I think his average this season is 43."

"That does sound impressive, Sir."

"Yes. Very strong off the front foot. And very elegant. Dare I say it, there's even a touch of David Gower about him. I sense that there's something else you haven't yet shared with me,

Inspector. By the way, there's no need to be so formal. Just call me Roy."

Inspector Goldman leaned back in his chair. "You're quite right ... Roy. But then, being a barrister, you'd be very familiar with the workings of the law. You know that I'd only come looking for you in the event of a troubling revelation."

"Troubling revelation?"

"I'm afraid so. We've already spoken at length to his estranged wife Melissa who had reported him missing, and to cut to the chase, we have now found his abandoned car in a car park in West Wittering. More disturbingly, there was a suicide note left in the glove compartment and clothes found on the beach are now undergoing lab tests with the forensics boys. But we have every reason to believe that they are the property of Mr Bartlett."

"Oh fuck. I wasn't expecting that, Inspector."

"I'm sorry to break all this to you so abruptly."

"This really is shocking news, Inspector. I mean, there were no outward signs of anything being terribly wrong. He always seemed in such good spirits. Were there any clues in the note as to why he was feeling this way?"

"No, I'm afraid not. It was pretty short. In fact, it's with a handwriting expert as we speak. We have to ascertain that it is his handwriting before we can rule out foul play."

"Of course."

"Did you know that he had been diagnosed with manic depression or what is now fashionably known as bipolar disorder?"

"Good heavens. No. I had no idea. Though I did know that he suffered from occasional bouts of depression. How did you discover that?"

"Melissa told us in passing and his GP has confirmed it."

"Do you think he really has topped himself?"

"We police inspectors never assume anything without evidence. Usually in circumstances like this, we'd expect a body to show up within a couple of days. In this case, we've alerted the coastal authorities to keep an eye out. Without a body, we are completely in the dark."

Roy stubbed out his cigarette and immediately lit another. It wasn't every day that you'd get informed by the police that someone you thought you knew pretty well had gone and topped themselves. As far as he understood, the whole divorce thing had been reasonably amicable — as amicable as these things could be. It hadn't been complicated by kids. They had been talking. Melissa had even lent the bugger money. So they must have still quite liked each other. None of this made any bloody sense. And then Roy had a nerve-wracking thought. *Who the fuck was going to open the batting?*

Chapter 12

Brian hadn't even removed his duffle coat when Angus appeared at the doorway with a tray of coffee and a couple of doughnuts. In his typewriter was a sheet of A4 that he'd clearly just been working on.

"Brian, take a pew and get your laughing gear around one of these beauties." He offered him one of the doughnuts.

"What's this in aid of then? Bit early for your birthday."

Angus grinned. "I just thought a celebration doughnut was in order."

"And what exactly are we celebrating?"

Angus whipped the sheet of A4 from his typewriter. "We are celebrating the fact that I've just gone and cracked the Simple TV brief." He handed Brian the script. "Feast your eyes on that and tell me it isn't bloody brilliant."

The script was short. Brian read it and couldn't believe what he was reading. He looked up, startled.

"You alright, mate? Looks like you've just seen a ghost."

"Sorry, Angus. But your script … Well, it isn't original."

"What are you talking about? There's no other TV commercial in the whole fucking history of advertising that features a white lily being sprayed with paint and perfume. Of course, it's totally fucking original."

Brian rummaged in the pocket of his duffle coat, pulled out a crumpled envelope and handed it to Angus, who unravelled it and read the neatly penned script that Brian had written.

"Jesus Christ." Angus couldn't believe it. Brian had written precisely the same script, almost word for word, describing a pristine white lily being sprayed with paint and perfume by robotic arms. Angus looked up as a shiver ran down his spine. "Fuck me … And there was me thinking that I was the only bloody genius in this place."

***

Magnus read the body copy through for the third time. Was he missing something? He was pretty sure he wasn't. Why in God's name had this perfectly acceptable but unmemorable piece of work been given the thumbs up by the jury? If a junior team had come up with it back at the ranch, he'd have politely told them to keep thinking. It wasn't terrible, but it certainly wasn't great. It probably wasn't even good. It was just okay at best. Surely, a press ad for the National Trust could do better than just say *Travel back in time?* The photograph of an old railway carriage was, admittedly, rather lovely. But this wasn't the photography category; it was the sodding copy category. He felt churlish as he gave it a score of 4. No sooner than he'd done so, a large man with a bushy dark beard tapped him on the shoulder.

"Hi there, stranger."

Magnus looked up into the face of the overbearing and larger-than-life bear of a man. "Sorry. Do I know you?"

"Do you know me? I should certainly fucking hope so. I guess it's the beard ..."

"Shit. It's Rob Mitchell, isn't it?" Rob's gravelly New York drawl was pretty unmistakable.

"The very same ... How the freakin' hell are you?"

"Oh, you know. Bearing up. I had no idea you were in London."

"Yeah. I've just been here a month working for that reprobate Slattery over at his new start-up." Rob then stopped in mid-sentence. "Oh, come on ... You Brits need to get fucking real."

"What's up? Do I have body odour or something?"

Rob laughed. "Fucking body odour, I can live with ... But four out of ten? For that piece of shit? You've got to be kidding me. I could do better with my knob and a pot of paint."

Rob was never one to mince his words or be backward in coming forward. Magnus had worked with him for a short while when he'd worked in New York. And Rob, in his view, was a brilliant copywriter — the kind of writer he'd love to hire, but GDR would have to win a few big accounts before they'd have enough in their war chest to afford him.

"Yeah, I know. You're right. It is a pile of elephant's dung and I've been pretty generous."

"I should fucking say so. But that's what I like about you Brits. You're all so fucking polite. Couldn't believe it when Slattery offered the job to a fat rude bastard like me."

Magnus laughed. "So, is it a permanent post?"

"Sure is. Wife and kids join next week. We've let the apartment in Manhattan and made an offer on a nice little place in Notting Hill. Schools are proving to be something of a nightmare though, but Sam is on the case." Rob leaned in closer to Magnus and then lowered his voice. "I've never had the pleasure of being a judge for these awards before but I reckon there's some real funny business going on here. It happens all the fucking time. I had to call it out last year when a couple of slimeballs tried to get some dumbass work through the jury at Cannes. If you back me up on this, Mags, I'm gonna let 'em have it big time — no holds barred. You with me, man?"

Magnus forced a grin and nodded nervously. "Yeah, of course."

"Good man. Nothing like putting a bunch of prize muppets back in their box."

Chapter 13

It was a strange fact of life that it was always the unseemly, the grotty, the downright depressing and run down that made the most interesting and strangely beautiful subjects. He zoomed into the detail of the Odeon's 1930s peeling paintwork and gently released the shutter. The midday sun was casting delicious shadows across its facade as an old dear with a tatty basket on wheels shuffled into the frame and suddenly Ben was gazing at an Edward Hopper composition that had magically come to life. It was a thing of sheer beauty. The motorised shutter sprang into action and froze the image countless times for posterity. He couldn't wait to get the negatives into the dark room to weave his magic.

And then it happened. The one single, innocent, inadvertent incident that would change everything in an instant. His dressing gown came undone. Why he was wearing a dressing gown and slippers on the seafront at Margate was a question he'd later find difficult to answer. But more difficult would be any kind of explanation for the lack of clothing beneath the dressing gown.

For once in his life, Benjamin Bartlett was exposing more than just film to the elements. To put no finer point on it, he was exposing his shrivelled genitalia to a 92-year-old who had, in fairness, seen her fair share of male genitalia over the years. She had, after all, been a GP in her youth. And she had enjoyed a healthy number of serious relationships with men including three husbands. But never before had she had the dubious pleasure of casting her eyes over the male anatomy at close quarters in a public place. Someone of a more sensitive nature might have found the experience a great deal more troubling, to say the least. It wasn't right. As far as she was concerned it was something up with which she would not put.

***

The tall, elegant man with silver hair and Savile Row suit was Robert Appleby. Magnus was on nodding terms with him and admired his work. He was arguably London's most respected copywriter for several reasons. Firstly, and most importantly, he had an impeccable reputation for writing the most eloquent, cogent and witty copy. No other writer in London had won as many accolades for writing. And then there was his demeanour. For an industry that had for years been looked down upon by the establishment as being something of an untamed and uncouth teenager with vulgar habits, Appleby had come to represent its antithesis. He was everything that the elite thought advertising wasn't. He was charming; he was urbane; he was smart; he was, in short, the perfect spokesman and figurehead for the entire industry. He was also the most senior of the judging panel whose duty, among other things, seemed to be corralling the troops and ensuring that all votes were cast in a fair and orderly fashion.

There was a tapping of a spoon on a champagne flute as Robert got to his feet. "Ladies and gentlemen. Or rather lady and gentlemen." The solitary female in the room, an art director named Louise Jennings, blushed as Robert bowed in her direction. "First of all, I'd like to thank the President of D&AD Johnny Boyce-Crumley for inviting me to preside over the judging of this year's D&AD Awards. It is a very great privilege and one I don't take lightly. This august body has come to represent the very best that our industry has to offer. It is, as you all know, gaining a reputation as one of the most revered awards bodies in the world. Entries this year have been at an all-time high and we should be proud that this country now seems to be leading the world for its creativity. And as someone who once had the great privilege of working for one of the most creative agencies that has ever sat on Madison Avenue, I can tell you that this never used to be the case. It was, of course, our American cousins who used to rule the roost; who called the shots; who received the lion's share of the adulation. How times have changed. Here on this small island, we've been rocking the boat and setting new standards. It is our job today to maintain these high standards. So I would urge you all to draw on your instincts. If you feel that the work you are being presented with doesn't merit an award or indeed a nomination, please do not feel compelled to give it your blessing. If some categories do not receive rewards, we will not be seen to be failing in our duties, but simply setting extremely high standards, which I'm pleased to say this organisation has become synonymous with. Once all categories have been judged, we will reconvene to review winning entrants and to consider an overall winner and a Lifetime Award. So before we go our separate ways, does anyone have any questions?"

"Yeah, sure." Rob Mitchell had got to his feet. "I'm one of your American cousins. And well, I don't mind at all if my English cousins get one over on me." This was greeted with a peal of nervous laughter. "Actually, I'm pretty darn proud of you guys. I want you to keep those standards frigging high. It's why I came here with my family to work full-time. So, yeah, I do have a question." He held up a board on which was mounted the National Trust double-page spread with the headline *Travel back in time*. "Would the arsewipes who nominated this piece of shite care to step forward?"

Chapter 14

"Would you like to explain, Mr Bartlett, why you were taking photographs on the seafront while displaying your wedding tackle to the whole world?" Ben looked at his shoes. He hadn't taken those yellow tablets for a few days now, and he knew that he had been behaving irrationally. He didn't have an answer; not a coherent one at any rate. He shrugged and then did something that he hadn't planned on doing. He began to sob.

PC Alan Newby always got given the nutcases. Last week he had to interview some old dear who'd been done for shoplifting cat food. Now he'd moved up in the world and was interviewing flashers. He handed Ben a box of tissues curiously emblazoned with bold macho typography that read MANSIZE. He wondered momentarily what WOMANSIZE would look like. "Here you go, Mr Bartlett. I'm going to leave the room for a few minutes to let you collect your thoughts and sort yourself out. Would you like a nice cup of tea and a Hobnob?"

Ben blew his nose into a tissue, nodded his head and found his voice. "Thank you. That's very kind. I wouldn't say no."

"Right you are."

***

Robert Appleby smiled wryly as the large American gesticulated and continued to rant about "sham awards" and "members patting themselves on the back".

As Magnus got to his feet and placed his arm around Rob's shoulder, Robert Appleby addressed the audience as if nothing had happened. He was not a man to be fazed easily. It was this easy charm that had helped him to successfully build a meaningful rapport with so many clients and establish his agency as one of London's most successful and revered.

"This is precisely the kind of passion I applaud. And frankly, I agree with Mr Mitchell here. This piece of work does not merit a place in our esteemed annual." He paused to pick up a glass of water, which he took time to sip. Appleby knew exactly how to make a dramatic point and keep his audience on tenterhooks. It was a well-honed performance and he knew it. "Look, we have to be passionate, honest and, yes, brutal ... But I would also remind my American cousin that we also have to be civil. This is not the place in which personal barbs and insults can be traded. Instead, I suggest we refer to our Constitution, which clearly stipulates that if two members of the judging panel deem any piece of work unworthy to be considered, then a secret ballot can be conducted by the judges in which said work must receive two-thirds of the vote to be accepted. Failure to do so will result in the work being rejected altogether."

***

Keith Millward lowered the window of the cab and lit a cigar. Ian smiled at his partner and could see that Keith was in a bullish mood. "You're relishing this, aren't you, Keith?"

Keith exhaled an enormous cloud of white cigar smoke out of the window, half of which blew back in. "Of course, I'm bloody relishing it. This could make us famous, Ian. Those two lads who are working on our brief were responsible for those fabulous commercials for real coal fires. My missus says she finds them funnier than the bleeding programmes, and do you know something? She's got a point." Ian laughed. Keith was right, of course. He admired his partner for trusting his instincts. Keith had always gone with his gut feeling; had always taken risks; and had always got it right. He'd deliberately kept the range of products small; kept the packaging design minimalist; and now he'd chosen to ditch this year's sales promotion and stick every penny of their marketing budget on TV with Channel 4. It was a big gamble. But if they got it right again, they could very well become a household name.

"I wonder what they'll come up with."

"Ian, as long as it's relevant and fucking memorable, do you know something? I don't particularly care."

"The two magic words relevant and memorable."

"You never were good at maths, Ian. It's three words. You left out the expletive."

They both laughed as the cab stopped on the corner of Great Pulteney Street and Keith paid the cabbie the fare plus a generous tip. Then he leaned back into the driver's window. "Don't suppose you like cigars, do you?"

The cabbie looked a bit taken aback. "I do like them as a matter of fact."

"Excellent ... Let me give you one of these. They are rather lovely. They're Cuban — the real McCoy." He pulled out a large silver tube from his jacket and handed it to the driver.

"Thanks a million. That looks lovely. I'll save it for my daughter's wedding."

"You do that. Au revoir."

Ian held open the door as Keith stepped out onto the pavement and was greeted by two unsavoury-looking individuals sitting on the polished tiled step of advertising agency Gordon Deedes Rutter. They were both inebriated and the larger of the two, who sported an impressive russet beard, raised his beer can. "May I propose a toast to your future fucking success and happiness?"

Keith smiled and looked at Ian. "It's an omen." Then he turned to the two vagrants. "That's extremely kind of you. And now, you must excuse us, we have an important meeting." They both stepped in an ungainly manner over the two figures while holding their noses as the pair smelt quite revolting.

***

"Hello. It's Keith and Ian, isn't it?"

"That's right. And you are Nicola, aren't you? Never forget a pretty face."

Nicola smiled, revealing her perfect pearly teeth. "I'll tell Bernard you're here. Would you like to take a seat?"

Keith picked up a copy of *The Times* and sank into a comfy leather sofa. *Giant of comedy dies on stage,* was the headline of the day and beneath the words, the distinctive features of Tommy Cooper in his trademark fez stared out of the newsprint. That was sad news, thought Keith. He'd seen the great man live many years ago at the Hackney Empire and had never laughed so much. He was one of those naturally and instinctively funny people that could make you laugh with a mere look or gesture.

"Hello, chaps. It's very nice to see you." Keith looked up from the newspaper. Bernard had stepped out of the lift and was already shaking Ian warmly by the hand. He approached Keith and did likewise. "Follow me. We're very excited about showing you our work." Bernard reopened the lift doors and they all stepped into its velvet-lined interior.

"And we," added Ian, "are very excited to be seeing it."

The boardroom was surprisingly large and accommodated an impressive boardroom table veneered with acres of walnut. Every ad agency in town had to have a sizeable boardroom table. It was a status symbol of sorts that gave clients the impression that the agency was a great deal more successful and heavyweight than the reality of its balance sheet would suggest. Around the walls were key frames from Angus and Brian's award-winning real coal fires television commercials, and an endless parade of framed award certificates.

Keith, Ian and Bernard took their seats in the middle of this vast ocean of wood and Bernard fiddled with the top of the coffee dispenser and did the honours. As he did so, Penny arrived with a tray of biscuits, and behind her, Angus and Brian made an entrance with a stack of white foam boards.

"Keith and Ian. Allow me to introduce Angus and Brian, our numero uno creative team." The two clients immediately rose to their feet and shook Angus and Brian by the hand.

"We are so pleased to meet you at long last. I do hope our short and pithy brief gave you something to get your creative teeth into."

Angus chuckled. "Wouldn't mind getting my creative teeth into a few of those biscuits. Bloody starving. I didn't have breakfast ..." He munched a couple of chocolate biscuits while offering Ian and Keith coffee. "It's very nice to meet you, too. And in answer to your question, your brief couldn't have been better. I only hope you both like the result."

Keith smiled amicably. "Let me say, Angus, that I have a feeling in my water that this is going to be a very significant moment in the history of our small brand and the hairs on the back of my neck are already tingling."

"Well, in that event, Keith," added Bernard, "I'm going to ask Brian here to take you through the work."

There was a nervous pause in the proceedings as Brian collated his boards and then placed a cassette into the sound system. "First of all, huge thanks for giving Angus and myself the opportunity to work on your brief, which to be honest, was a dream brief for any creative team to have a crack at. And the very strange thing is that both Angus and I had the very same idea independently. I had it while in the bath in my flat in Hampstead while the same idea popped into Angus's head while he was having a post-coital cigarette in Wimbledon."

Keith roared with laughter and offered Angus a cigar. "You may like to try a post-coital cigar next time."

Brian placed the first keyframe of his storyboard on the presentation wall. It displayed a beautiful white lily. "Imagine if you will a beautifully lit white lily in a natural environment." He then revealed the second keyframe, showing a mechanical robotic arm with a spray gun. "And now imagine said flower being sprayed with colouring and perfume by two robotic arms. A voice-over would read the following words: 'When something is as pure and natural as this, would you add artificial colouring? Would you add perfume? Neither would we.' And then we'd fade to the packshot and our end line: *Not perfumed. Not coloured. Just kind.*" Brian then switched on the sound system. "And this is a piece of music we've had composed by Lord David Dundas in the style of Erik Satie. We think this should work pretty well when it's actually composed to picture." He pressed the play button and the resonant sound of Lord Dundas's Steinway broke the silence. The cassette clicked itself off at the end of the short demo and they all sat in silence for what seemed to Angus like an eternity. Keith eventually got to his feet and paced over to Brian and gave him an enormous bear hug and kissed him extravagantly on both cheeks. He repeated this to all three of them. It was the first time Bernard had ever been kissed by a client and the experience was strangely embarrassing.

"Gentlemen. I can honestly say that I am very rarely left speechless. But this presentation leaves me bereft of words." Keith picked up the board with the lily beautifully rendered in Magic Marker. "There is nothing to add. It is perfection personified. Please, please go away and make it happen. I am in your very capable hands. And I thank you profusely."

Bernard smiled at Brian and Angus. The boys had gone and cracked it. They were in business. He couldn't wait to get on the phone and break the news to Magnus.

Angus stepped forward and shook Keith vigorously by the hand. "Thank you so much, Keith. But I warn you, if you kiss me again like that, I might have to sue you for sexual assault." They both locked eyes for a nano-second and then roared with laughter.

Chapter 15

"Maggers ... It's the only way to deal with arseholes. I'm sorry if I embarrassed you. You know, we Brooklynites say it how it is. You Brits may go in for clandestine stuff and stab each other in the back. But in Brooklyn, we don't mess about — we stab in the front." Rob sank back into the seat of the cab and took a swig from his hip flask as the cab lurched around a corner.

Magnus chuckled. He liked Rob but he was something of an embarrassment. "No need to apologise, Rob. And it wasn't the least bit embarrassing. And look, it got the desired result."

"Yeah. I have to say. I like that fella Robert. To put it in English parlance, I like the cut of the guy's jib." They both laughed.

"He's a good egg," said Magnus. "I don't know him, but I know from people who've worked with him that he's a very decent bloke and deeply religious by all accounts."

"Is that right? It figures. I guess things might have got a great deal more heated had he not handled things as diplomatically as he did. And the son of a gun writes like a frigging demon."

Magnus nodded. He'd read every piece of copy written by Robert Appleby and was in awe of the man.

"I'm surprised he hasn't written a novel yet," continued Rob. "I mean if that copywriter guy who wrote *Midnight's Children* ... What's his name?"

"Salman Rushdie, I believe."

"Yeah, that's the guy. Well, if he can write a novel without having written anything particularly memorable for this industry, just imagine what this Appleby guy might be capable of."

"You're not wrong. Perhaps when he has time away from his agency, he will. I'd certainly be one of the first to read it."

"Yeah, me too."

***

Benjamin Bartlett had been kept waiting in that bare room for what seemed like hours. When the door finally did open, he was surprised and a little worried to see the face of a more senior-looking police officer.

The man, who must have been in his late forties or early fifties, pulled up a chair and sat down.

"Mr Bartlett. I have good news and bad news. I'll give you the good news first, shall I?"

Benjamin nodded.

"Well, the good news is that on this occasion, you are being released without charge. However, the bad news is this: you have committed a serious offence. To be more precise, three serious offences. You have staged your own false demise; exposed yourself on Margate seafront; and wasted police time. I, for one, don't appreciate having my time wasted, Mr Bartlett. I have far better things to do than chase after people like you. And the Kent constabulary take a very dim view of those who waste police time. As a result of your antics, you're a whisker away from a criminal record."

Chapter 16

Chaz carefully tied the knot in his silk tie and placed the matching silk handkerchief in his breast pocket. He was no longer Chaz from the Dog and Duck, but Charles Wainwright from Sevenoaks. He placed the tortoiseshell-framed spectacles with clear glass on his nose and the silver cigarette case in his jacket pocket.

The Rolls Royce Silver Cloud was waiting for him in the usual spot. It had seen better days and was no longer hired out for weddings, but it never failed to impress his aged clients. He had three ports of call, all of them in Hove.

He loved this old car. It may have seen over twenty years of service to the great and the good but its engine still purred like a thoroughbred. He put himself in the right frame of mind by tuning the radio to Radio Three. The BBC was playing a recording of the previous evening's concert at the Barbican in its Leonard Bernstein Festival. The London Philharmonic were playing Gershwin's Rhapsody in Blue under the baton of a young conductor named Bramwell Tovey, who had apparently stepped in at the last moment when the programme's official conductor had become ill. Bernstein, the great maestro himself, had actually been in the audience. During the interval, the BBC played a short interview with the young Tovey, who amusingly explained that he had been ironing when he received the frantic call from the Director of the London Philharmonic who had asked if he'd be available to step in. Tovey said he had to take a deep breath and pretend for a few moments that he had to consult his less-than-busy diary, before replying that he could probably manage it. He couldn't believe his luck.

By the time Charles had reached Hove, it was midday. He switched off the radio and the ignition and pulled up the handbrake. The road in which his new client lived looked most promising. Late Victorian, possibly Edwardian, semis, most of which retained their original sash windows and elaborate front doors housing stained-glass panels. This was the land of professionals; middle-class accountants, solicitors, bankers, and the like. He looked in the mirror and straightened his tie. Then he collected his leather attaché case with his notepads and Sotheby's catalogues from the back seat.

A young West Indian woman answered the door. She was wearing a blue nurse's uniform and was clearly a live-in carer.

"Good afternoon. I assume you are Charles Wainwright?"

Charles nodded and smiled. "I certainly am. It's very nice to meet you."

"Henry is expecting you. Follow me, please."

He followed the carer through a long hallway of tessellated Edwardian floor tiles that formed geometric patterns in terracotta, ochre, blue and white that led into an attractive dining room with French doors that looked out onto a tranquil walled garden. The place was stuffed with antiques. There were late eighteenth-century chairs, several nice-looking clocks, a fair number of porcelain pieces from the Meissen factory and a few promising Ming vases. There were plenty of original paintings adorning the walls, too, including a couple of Myles Birket Foster watercolours. Charles was positively salivating before he even got a chance to sit down at the table that had already been prepared for tea.

Henry was sitting at the table and gestured to the seat opposite him. "Mr Wainwright. Do take a seat. It's very nice to meet you in person and it's very good of you to make the journey from Sevenoaks."

Charles raised his hand. "Don't mention it. It's my pleasure."

Henry looked up at his carer. "Thank you, Marcia. That will be all. You can leave me with Mr Wainwright and close the door behind you."

Marcia didn't like the look of this Charles Wainwright. He was far too smarmy for her liking. She was protective of Henry who had been a very good and kind employer. She didn't want him to get taken in by some unscrupulous con man. And these days, since his wife had passed away, he'd become far too trusting and accepting of people and services in general. She reluctantly closed the door and retreated to the kitchen where she made herself a strong mug of black coffee.

"I'll be honest with you, Mr Wainwright. I am planning to sell this place and am getting my affairs in order. I haven't told Marcia or my family, because ... well because they'd be understandably upset. You see, Mr Wainwright, when you get to my age, you have to be realistic and plan for your eventual demise. Thank God I still have my marbles, and I can do all these things, even though my body doesn't always allow me to do the things I'd dearly love to do — like gardening."

Charles smiled benignly. This was all looking rather wonderful. The old man was looking to sell everything presumably and he'd have a chance to do rather nicely if he played his cards right. It was very tempting to steal a couple of small items but even he now realised that would be extremely foolish in the circumstances. There was too much at stake here. Henry was a bright old bird — he was nobody's fool. He could give him some fair prices for the furniture and some of the porcelain. Impress him with his knowledge. But he could do very nicely on the watercolours and clocks.

"What I'd like from you, Mr Wainwright, is a valuation of all the items of value in the house. So once you finish your tea, please do take your time to draw up an inventory and give me a valuation in your own time. By releasing the equity in this place and my assets I intend to set up a trust fund for my grandchildren. I'd like to help them all financially when I finally shuffle off this mortal coil."

"That's not a problem, Mr ..."

"The name is Sullivan, Henry Sullivan. But you can just call me Henry."

"Well, Henry. I will do just that and unlike Sotheby's, who will charge you around 12 per cent in commission, I won't charge you anything. And as you know, I pay in cash."

"Excellent ... Now, tell me. As an expert, which items in this place excite you the most, Mr Wainwright?"

Charles knew that he was being tested. The old man obviously knew what he had. What he wouldn't know, of course, was their true market value. "Well, Henry. I do like the look of your Meissen and George Hepplewhite chairs. Very nice examples, if I may say so. And very desirable in the current market. Unfortunately, the market for Victorian watercolours has fallen quite considerably in recent years. They just aren't as fashionable as they once were. And, of course, the Birket Fosters, while rather charming, are only limited-edition prints." The truth of the matter was that while they may have been perfectly collectable, in terms of value, the porcelain and furniture were nowhere near as valuable as the Birket Foster watercolours, which were, in fact, highly valuable originals in their original frames. Charles couldn't help himself from lying. It was a risky strategy but this was where he could make a killing. He knew perfectly well that Birket Fosters were highly sought-after in America and were currently going for insane prices through Sotheby's and Bonhams.

"That's very interesting, Mr Wainwright. I've always admired the furniture. And you are quite right. They are George Hepplewhite. They belonged to my father-in-law. As for the art, I'm no expert, but you clearly know your onions."

Charles finished his tea and opened his attaché case. "If it's alright by you, Henry, I will just draw up an inventory now, room by room. Is there anything upstairs?"

Henry shook his head. "No. Everything upstairs will go to my children or charity. And the Steinway is going to Sussex University."

It was a shame about the Steinway. Charles had done a few nice deals on Steinways and Bechsteins. He knew a dealer that paid very good prices for their private international clients.

He got to his feet and took a pen and notepad from his case. "I'll get on then, Henry. Shouldn't take me more than an hour to get an inventory together. Then give me a few days and I'll get back to you with a price. I can certainly take everything off your hands and promise you a tidy sum."

"Excellent. Now, you must excuse me. I need to have my afternoon nap." He picked up a silver bell and rang it and within seconds Marcia appeared at the door. "Marcia, I am ready for my afternoon nap. Mr Wainwright here is going to put together his inventory. When he's done, could you let him out, please?" She smiled. "It was very nice meeting you, Charles. I look forward to hearing back from you in due course. Good day."

By the time Charles had finished his inventory, he'd filled up four sides of a lined A4 pad with tightly written descriptions. His first impressions had been pretty accurate. The paintings were all very sellable. And a few notable pieces including the Birket Foster watercolours would easily fetch several thousand each at Sotheby's. He put away his notepad and exchanged pleasantries with Marcia who was clearly just going through the motions. She obviously didn't trust him. He could tell.

Back in the car, his mind turned to that deceitful little shit Ben Bartlett. It was only four days ago that the photographer had threatened him with going to the police, but Chaz had no intention of paying the bastard. If the little toe rag did go to the police, Chaz would be in serious trouble. He'd already been inside for a couple of years for fraud. Blackmailing a man of the cloth might well put him away for considerably longer. He was going to have to find a way to shut the sod up one way or another. The little git may have done a runner. But he wasn't going to evade Chaz that easily.

Chapter 17

"Have you seen Brian?"

Penny looked up from her desk. "Oh, I think he was down with Joan from Archives ten minutes ago. Probably still there."

Angus smiled. "Great. I'll pop down."

Penny was right. She usually was. Brian was engrossed in an article by *Campaign* magazine.

"Hi, guv'nor."

Brian looked over the magazine. "Hi, Aggers. Take a look at this." He threw over the magazine and Angus took a look. The headline read: *Photographer arrested by police for indecent exposure.* Angus continued reading.

This magazine has learnt that the award-winning advertising photographer Benjamin Bartlett was recently arrested and later released by police for staging his own death and then exposing himself on the seafront in Margate. Sally Withers takes up the story.

I'm sitting in the studio of Benjamin Bartlett, better known for his unusual photographic techniques and award-winning campaigns for the likes of Arctic Lite and the English Tourist Board. He is well presented in a pair of Levi 501s, Nike trainers and a cashmere pullover. "So how have the last few weeks been?" I ask him. He smiles knowingly and sips at a glass of something non-alcoholic. "It's been pretty tough. I'm what doctors call a classic manic depressive", he says. He then goes on to describe the condition in some detail. Apparently, his mood swings can be fairly dramatic, to say the least. When he's high, he's likely to go to lots of parties; is filled with boundless enthusiasm and tends to drink too much. When he's low, he can sink into a very deep depression, and not get out of bed for days. "Things got to something of a crisis point a few weeks back," he explains. "I began to get irrational. And I forgot to take my medication. And things got so bad that I seriously contemplated suicide. I was being totally irrational. And to be honest, I didn't really know what I was doing." He goes on to explain that having left a suicide note in the car at West Wittering, he didn't have the guts to actually drown himself and instead dragged himself off to Margate where he was brought up as a kid, and visited his mum who he hadn't seen for some while.

"Seeing my mum again was certainly good for me," he says. "Seeing her seemed to bring about a mood swing and stopped me feeling so bloody depressed."

He takes another sip from his glass and looks at me embarrassingly. "But I know what you're itching to ask." I say nothing. "You want to know how on earth I got arrested for indecent exposure. And I don't blame you. It's a good question. If I were you I'd certainly want to ask it. And the answer is pretty disappointing I'm afraid." He goes on to explain that though the depression had obviously lifted, he was still in a pretty delicate state and was in something of a "daydream". He had enthusiastically set out with his camera and lenses and had become entirely focused on capturing some beautiful arty shots. So much so that he hadn't even registered that he was wearing nothing more than a dressing gown and a pair of slippers. When a gust of wind caused his dressing gown to blow open, he was oblivious to the fact that he'd just gone and exposed himself to a passer-by. "It was only when I was arrested that I realised what had happened," he adds.

At first, the police didn't seem to believe him, but they gradually came round to accepting his account of events. "They even went as far as getting my film developed to see what I'd been photographing," he adds. "When they saw the results, I think they were impressed. And one of the junior officers asked me if I'd used filters to get the effects."

"Did you?" I venture.

He taps his nose and smiles. "That would be telling."

There were several more paragraphs about his work and a selection of images, some of which were of Margate. Angus had read enough. "Interesting story. Magnus will be interested in reading it as he used him for the Long Life Beer campaign."

Brian nodded. "Yeah. Nice work, too. I don't suppose this piece will do him any harm. I'll leave it on Magnus's desk."

***

Roy sat in the studio, glass of Rioja in hand. "I can't tell you how relieved I am to be sitting here with you, mate."

Ben topped up his own glass. "Thanks, Roy. I appreciate that, and I'm sorry to have caused so much worry. Most people in my position wouldn't fuck things up as badly as me. I mean, I had it all going for me on paper — lovely, successful wife; great job doing what I love; big bloody house on a nice road. Wasn't enough to keep me out of the funny farm, though, was it?"

"Not sure that I'd describe The Priory as a funny farm. It's more like a luxury hotel. Bet the food was good."

"It was actually. And in fairness, I needed those couple of weeks there. They've put me on different medication, and the therapist was really good. Surprisingly good to be perfectly honest. I didn't want to go but my GP persuaded me. And Melissa, bless her, footed the bill. It sounds strange, but I don't even know why we're getting divorced."

Roy wasn't entirely sure either. Melissa was bloody gorgeous and smart. He smiled and raised his glass. "I think what you need is a cricket match, mate."

"I'll drink to that."

"Look, I know it might be a bit premature, but can I persuade you to put your whites on this Sunday? We're playing Worcester College, Oxford on their ground."

Ben chuckled. "Yeah. Thanks, I'd love that."

"You don't have to open the innings. You can bat down the order if you prefer."

"No. Sod that. I'll open the innings. Put me down for Sunday, Roy. I'll be there. I promise."

"Good man. There'll be a huge sigh of relief back at base camp, I can tell you. We've missed you, Ben."

"Thanks, Roy. You know, this whole episode hasn't done me any harm. Quite the reverse. Ever since I did that interview for

Campaign magazine, that bloody phone hasn't stopped ringing. I've been getting so many jobs from agencies that I've had to take on a PA."

"Sounds like a nice problem to have. I know the feeling — being a fellow freelancer."

"I didn't know barristers were freelancers."

"Oh, yes, we're all self-employed. Unless we work for the government or the Crown Prosecution Service."

"But you don't have the kind of money worries some of us have."

"Lack of work may not hurt my finances, but it would certainly bruise the old ego."

"Ego? I don't think I have one of those. Used to have one once."

Chapter 18

Brian's car arrived at 8.30 and the driver woke them both up when he thumped on the front door. Linda was a light sleeper but they had both managed to sleep through the radio alarm clock, which was still playing Radio Four's *Today* programme.

"Brian. Wake up! Your car's here. We've overslept."

He looked at her through bleary eyes. Her hair was tousled, but she looked sultry and magnificent. He was a lucky blighter. "Oh, bugger." He yawned. "Did I ever tell you how beautiful you look in the morning?"

"Come on, you silly sod. Get yourself into the bathroom. I'll take the door."

She threw on Brian's silk dressing gown and unlocked the front door.

A balding man in a black leather jacket smiled at her. "Hello, darlin'. Car for Brian Finkle."

"He'll be with you in a couple of minutes. I'm afraid we're running a bit late. Can I offer you a coffee?" The man looked a little nonplussed. "Go on. We've got a fancy new machine. Makes a lovely brew."

"Oh. If you insist. I'll have a splash of milk and one sugar."

"Come in and take a pew."

The driver took a seat at the kitchen table. "Nice place you have here."

"Thanks. We only moved in a couple of months ago. The previous owners were interior designers, so we have them to thank."

"I know these roads like the back of my hand."

"My brother did The Knowledge. I know what it's like. You have to have a photographic memory to pass that thing."

"Oh, I wasn't really referring to that ... I was brought up in Hampstead as a kid. So it's my stomping ground. We used to live in Church Row."

She placed a mug of coffee on the table. "Wow. That's dead posh."

"Thanks, luv. That's lovely." He took a sip. "Yeah. It was very posh. We had nannies, went to private schools, and even had our own chef. Didn't last though." He took another sip at the coffee and looked a touch wistful. "The old man was a big shot in the publishing game, but he was also a big drinker and gambler, and when the drink finally killed him, all his chickens came home to roost. He owed everyone including the banks so much money that poor old mum couldn't begin to settle the debt. And to make matters even worse, he hadn't even left a will. So to cut a long story short, we ended up living in a council house in Deptford. Still, that's life, eh?"

Linda raised her eyebrows. "That's some rollercoaster ride."

The sound of a closing door announced the arrival of Brian in the doorway clasping a small leather holdall. "Hi there. Sorry to keep you waiting. We'd better make a move. I have a commercial to make." He kissed Linda and followed the driver out into the street.

***

The taxi pulled up outside the studio and Brian thanked the driver.

Brooks Fulford Cramer Seresin, otherwise known as BFCS, was housed in the Paddington Basin, overlooking a dog-leg of dirty canal water that formed part of the Grand Union Canal that sat south of the more desirable Little Venice. The purpose-built studio was incongruous among the tumbledown warehousing left over from the Industrial Revolution and the Golden Age of canals. Brian stepped through the large glass doors into the cool minimalist white interior. It was a bit like walking into an art gallery.

Studio Two was a hive of activity and Len was orchestrating everything from the eye-piece of his sizeable camera. While the lighting cameraman was adjusting the position of lights, model makers added the final touches to a row of larger-than-life model lilies.

"Good morning, Brian. Would you like to take a look through the camera?" Len vacated his seat and Brian gratefully obliged.

"Oh, that's very nice, Len. How do you get that lovely soft background? It's much nicer through the lens."

"I'm glad you like that. We've applied a thin film of Vaseline to the lens. It's an old Hollywood trick. I'm just going to try a few different things with the lighting, but we're not far off. Why don't you join your partner in crime upstairs for breakfast? I recommend the bacon rolls — they're a bit special."

"Oooh, now you're talking. I didn't have breakfast. Oh, and by the way, Len. We've chosen Joanna Lumley for the voice-over."

Len laughed. "My goodness. I photographed her back in the day when I was a stills photographer and she was a young model. We were both starting out in our respective careers. I don't suppose she'll remember me. It's a good choice. I think her voice will work really well with the visuals."

The staff canteen was large, chic and looked out onto the canal. Angus was ensconced in the far corner with a pad, a cup of coffee and an empty plate.

"Morning, squire."

Angus looked up. "Afternoon. Nice of you to grace us with your presence. I was toying with the idea of going downstairs and playing at art director."

"Alright. I'm a bit late, I know. But it's all under control down there. They won't be shooting for a little while yet. Len is still experimenting with the lighting."

"I'm only teasing, mate. I've only been here ten minutes myself. Go and grab yourself a bacon butty. They are bloody marvellous."

"Looks like you're doing some work there."

"I had an idea last night for a pitch brief that's coming our way. Bernard told me about it last night in the pub. Go and get your breakfast first and I'll fill you in."

Brian took his place in a short queue at the counter. You could tell this was a creative environment. The dress code seemed to be denim jeans and t-shirts. By the time Brian had returned with his breakfast, Angus had laid a couple of A4 sheets of unintelligible scribbles on the table. "The pitch is for a burglar alarm system called Big Brother that is apparently really clever and uses the very latest motion sensors with infrared technology. So here's my very simple idea, which takes the form of a testimonial. We show a series of men being interviewed about the product. We see their faces in close-up. None of them have a good word to say about it and tell the viewer not to bother. One says it's daylight robbery. Another one says it's a complete waste of time. And the last one begrudgingly admits that he does feel more secure now. Then the camera pulls back and reveals that they are all convicted burglars in prison. And here's our endline: *Big Brother. As tested by experts.*"

Brian laughed. "I love it, Angus. I think casting will be really important though. We don't want to give the joke away. They have to look like really nice, loveable old boys or girls for that matter. The reveal has to be a big surprise."

Angus nodded. "I agree entirely, Brian."

"In fact, why don't we approach that mad flashing photographer Ben Bartlett? I heard on the grapevine that he wants to get into directing. I reckon we could persuade him to do us a test film for the pitch on the basis of being given the real job if we end up winning it."

"You're not just a pretty face, Finkle. That's a great idea. We'll need to run it past Magnus first. But I can't see why he'd say no. Why don't we get a cab over to Bartlett's studio later and sound him out now and get ahead of the game because he's going to need time to set all this up, and he's likely to be busy on other jobs?"

Brian nodded. "Yeah. You're right. Time is of the essence."

"I feel good about this one, Brian. Do you fancy a second breakfast by way of a celebration?"

"Oh, go on then."

Chapter 19

Ben stared at the telephone for some while. His palms were sweaty, his heart was racing, and he thought he was having some kind of anxiety attack. He wasn't good at this. He picked up the phone and dialled the number he'd taken down from the telephone directory. The phone rang for a few seconds and was then picked up.

"Hello. You are through to Dr Simon Granger at the Vicarage ... Hello ... Hello ... Is anybody there?" All Simon could hear was heavy breathing. He'd had these perverts call him in the past. He was mystified why anyone would find vicars and cassocks in the least bit erotic. He was about to hang up but was deterred from doing so by a faltering voice.

"Look ... You don't know me. And it's best you don't know who I am. But I have some information for you. Valuable information. I'm not looking for payment. I just want to help you. I just want to do the right thing ..."

Chapter 20

"Would Madam care to order?"

Melissa was feeling irritated. It wasn't even her idea to come here.

"No. I'm waiting for my husband. He should have been here by now."

The waiter bowed and returned to the kitchen.

She'd only spoken to him once on the phone since he'd left The Priory and he'd sounded perfectly together. They may have been divorcing but the truth of the matter was that they were still friends. A part of her still quite liked him. Yes, he could be insufferable and stubborn but she didn't want him to suffer from some kind of mental breakdown or whatever it was he was going through. And there were times when she wondered if the divorce had been the straw that broke the camel's back. Admittedly, that thought alone did make her feel a tad guilty. Was she a genuinely caring person or was she simply unable and unwilling to accept that she might be the reason for his mental state? When she thought he might have topped himself, she really did begin to feel culpable. And it genuinely hurt. She didn't want to feel that any more. She wanted to do the right thing. That's why she was sitting here, after all. So why in God's name couldn't that prick of a husband do the same?

Chapter 21

"Sarge. I've got that Melissa Bartlett on the phone. You're not going to believe this, but her husband's disappeared off the radar again."

Sergeant Morris Dixon looked heavenward. "If he's wasting police time again, Inspector Goldman is going to throw the book at him. And it won't be any old book. I'm talking bloody *War and Peace*. The hardback version in oversized print for the visually impaired."

Chapter 22

"I know you're not much of a jazz fan, Aggers, but do you and Sam fancy joining Linda and me next Tuesday night at Ronnie Scott's?"

Angus was gazing out of the window of the studio's canteen at nothing in particular. He was in the process of writing copy for a trade advertisement for the Solid Fuel Advisory Service and was trying without much luck to think of a witty endline.

"Cheers, mate. Actually, Sam is partial to a bit of jazz. I've never been to Ronnie Scott's. It will be an education. I gather Ronnie himself often does a bit of a stand-up routine between gigs."

"Yeah. Always the same gags. But he tells them well in his own laconic way."

"Out of interest, who's playing? Not that I'll be familiar with them. But Sam might be."

"A guy called Joe Pass. He's quite probably the world's greatest living jazz guitarist. And he's being accompanied by Oscar Peterson on piano."

"Is that *the* Oscar Peterson?"

"Certainly is."

"Christ. Even I've heard of him. I've seen him on the telly box."

"He always gets a full house at Ronnie's. So you're in luck."

"That's really good of you … I'm sure Sam will be more than up for it. How's Len getting on downstairs by the way?"

"Pretty well. They're just setting up the mechanical arms, which look terrific. And the lilies are on some kind of spring system — so when they get sprayed they sway slightly like real lilies. Bloody clever and looks totally convincing."

"Sounds great. I'll go down in a bit and have a look. I spoke to Magnus earlier. He reckons we should just go over to

Bartlett's studio when we can get away and introduce ourselves and sound him out about the Big Brother script. If he's not in the studio, there's a good chance we'll find him in the boozer opposite. What do you reckon?"

"Why not? The sooner we get to talk to him the better ... Looks like you're busy there. Have you been writing copy?"

"Yeah. It's for that trade ad we did for solid fuel. You know, the one with the tongue-in-cheek headline that says: *'Ever since the dawn of civilisation, man has been attracted to fire.'* I've pretty much written it but just need a suitable end line."

Brian grinned.

"You've thought of one, haven't you? Come on, Finklebrain. Spit it out."

"It's pretty terrible. You're going to hate it."

"Let me be the judge of that."

"Okay. How about: *Real fires. They're selling like hot caves?*"

"Finkle, has anyone ever told you that you're a bloody genius?"

***

"Cheers, Magnus." Bernard tapped champagne glasses with Magnus. Their presentation to Psion had been well received. The clients were a couple of very smart South African computer geeks who had created the world's first hand-held computer. And they desperately wanted to tell the world about it with a TV commercial.

When they last met, the company hadn't even finalised the name and logo. But now that had all been signed off and approved. It was to be called the Psion Organiser and the logo had been created from a specially designed futuristic typeface.

Magnus had talked them through the script; played a demo track of Roy Plomley reading the voice-over; and finally played a video of a comic actor pretending to carry a computer system in his pocket.

He had worried that these two computer nerds wouldn't have a sense of humour and having shown them the idea, the lack of laughter might have confirmed his suspicions. But this wasn't the case at all. They were very happy with the script, the choice of Roy Plomley for the voice, and even the choice of actor — Walter Zerlin Junior, otherwise known as Robert Conway. Conway actually led a double life by being a barrister during the day and a stand-up comedian by night. Angus and Brian had introduced Magnus to Robert some months earlier and they had hit it off. Besides writing comedy, Conway was a natural clown and had put together an amusing little video of himself struggling to carry an imaginary computer system in his trouser pocket.

"To be perfectly honest, Magnus," said Bernard, "those two coves are pretty strange, aren't they? I mean, how on earth can you sit through Conway's antics and not even smile?"

Magnus nodded. "I agree. I thought they hated every minute of the thing. I don't think they are humourless, but for some curious reason, they obviously don't like to show it. Still, looks like we're in business."

"How challenging is their tiny production budget going to be?"

Angus smiled. "I knew you'd ask that, and it's a fair question. But I was being totally sincere when I told them that it wasn't going to pose a problem. There are plenty of really talented young directors in this city who'd give their eye-teeth to shoot a half-decent commercial from a respected creative agency at cost price for their showreel. And we're already saving ourselves a small fortune by not using a celebrity comedian. Robert is brilliant and isn't going to cost us very much at all. It could make his comedy career. By the way, I'm seeing him later. He wants to introduce me to another fellow comedian who is appearing in his farces at the Donmar Warehouse. He says I've got to see him. Apparently, he's a scream. Why don't you join us?"

"Thanks. I'd love to. What's the other guy's name?" asked Bernard.

"Good question. He did tell me ... Julian, yeah, that's it. Julian Clary."

Chapter 23

"No, don't be silly chaps. There's absolutely no need for you to be here any longer. Everything, as you can see, is under control. I'm just going to do one more take of the grabber picking up the perfume bottle and squeezing the puffer. We'll have a look at the rushes in the morning. But as far as I'm concerned, everything is going to plan. We have plenty of time to shoot five more set-ups tomorrow including the packshot. It's going to be a lovely piece of work."

Brian felt like he really was in safe hands. What a top bloke Len was. Not only was he a perfectionist with a great eye and sensibility, he understood the power of a good idea. You only had to look at his showreel. There wasn't a single piece of work there that didn't revolve around a strong idea. And that was something that few directors were able to boast. Even some of the best in the business would stick an ad on their reel that may have looked gorgeous but offered absolutely nothing to stimulate the grey matter. Len was smarter than that. He was also, needless to say, one of the nicest directors you could ever wish to work with.

Brian nodded. "Thanks, Len. You're a star."

"My pleasure. You run along now. I'll see you both in the morning."

***

"Hello ... Hello ..." Magnus pushed all his loose change into the pay phone and heard electronic bleeps on the other end of the line.

"Hello. You are through to Robert Conway's answer machine. Robert Conway is a full-time barrister available to take on all your litigation work. As night falls, however, Robert Conway vacates his body for his alter ego Walter Zerlin Junior. Walter, as you might imagine, is not a barrister. He is an outrageous stand-up comedian and comedy writer. He is available for all occasions including private parties, hen nights and Bar Mitzvahs ..." Magnus was about to leave a message when there was a sudden clicking noise on the line and a familiar voice rang out.

"Hello there. Terribly sorry about that. My cleaner accidentally put the answering machine on when dusting. How can I help?"

"Robert, it's Magnus here. Sorry to call you so late."

"That's okay Magnus. How are things?"

"All's well thanks. And I have good news ... The client wants to go ahead with the commercial, and they liked your performance."

"Oh, that's fantastic, Magnus. How exciting."

"The only snag is that we're working with a pretty tight budget as the client is pouring most of their hard-earned income on TV media, which doesn't come cheap even on Channel 4. But it's not going to be an insurmountable hurdle. I'm confident that we can strike a deal with an up-and-coming director."

"Thanks for letting me know, Magnus. Now where is this curry house that we're meeting at?"

"It's a lovely little place in East Finchley High Street called Cochin. It's South Indian, which I find less oily."

"As an advertising exec, I thought you'd be alright with a bit of oil — particularly the snake variety."

"Very funny."

Chapter 24

By the time the taxi pulled into the kerb, the light was beginning to fade and the street lights were coming on. Angus and Brian jumped out of the cab and headed for Bartlett's studio just off the King's Road.

"Feels a bit odd just dropping in like this, don't you think?" Brian had a point, but Magnus had been fairly clear when he'd spoken to Angus.

"I know what you mean," replied Angus. "It had occurred to me, too. But it's the kind of way Magnus deals with things, isn't it? He likes to grab the bull by the horns. And I guess he wants us to do likewise." As he spoke, he pressed the door buzzer. There were no visible lights on and they waited in silence. "Shall I ring again for longer maybe?" Brian nodded. And Angus obliged. Still no signs of life. Angus put his hands to the glass panel in a vain attempt to see if he could discern anything inside, and in doing so, the door opened. They looked at each other and without saying anything entered and closed the door behind them.

It was dark in the entrance lobby. Angus raised his voice. "Hello. Anyone at home?" There was no answer. Brian flicked on a light switch and the lights to the whole studio flooded the place with bright white light. The studio was enormous and was set up with a room set of an old Victorian library. There was a mug of coffee on the side that was still lukewarm.

"Why on earth was the door left open? Anyone could just nick all this equipment. It must be worth a fortune."

Angus shrugged. "Beats me. Shall we check out the pub opposite? Magnus says he spends most of his time over there when he's not doing a shoot."

Brian was distracted by the room set. "Look at this, Aggers." He pulled out a row of antique books from one of the shelves. It was nothing more than a hollow shell displaying a row of fake leather book spines. "How clever is that?" But not everything was fake. There was an original Victorian desk and a large ornate cupboard with delicate inlay work. Brian ran his index finger down the glass-like French polished surface and for some inexplicable reason opened the cupboard door. He wished he hadn't, because there in front of him no more than inches from his nose was the pale, grimacing face of Benjamin Bartlett. His eyes were almost popping out of his head and he looked in excruciating pain. He was hanging by the neck and was clearly dead.

"Fuck!"

Angus immediately took a look. "Jesus fucking wept. He's either topped himself or been murdered, Brian." He then whispered. "And if he's been murdered, who's to say the murderer isn't still here?"

"Stay calm. We're leaving now. We're going over to the pub. And we're going to phone the police."

"But we will be suspects, Brian."

"Yeah, I know. But we have no choice. And we have alibis. The studio and that cab driver will vouch for us. We can't pretend we haven't seen his body,"

"You're right. Let's do it."

"Oh, shit."

"What's up?"

"I think I'm going to be sick."

***

"So that's one Chicken Dhansak, one Chicken Tikka Masala, one Biryani, and one Lamb Tandoori with pilau rice for four, a plate of poppadoms and four Kingfisher beers."

Magnus nodded and thanked the waiter and Robert Conway's friend Julian Clary gave him a knowing smile. "Now that's what I call Nirvana."

The waiter looked a little perplexed, "Sorry, Sir. This dish Nirvana we don't have."

"No, I'm sorry. It's just a figure of speech. We're fine. That's everything. Thank you."

The waiter smiled and bowed. As soon as he'd disappeared they all laughed. Bernard leaned forward and grinned at Julian. "If it is the King Prawn Nirvana that you will be wanting, allow me to recommend the utopian rice. A veritable match made in heaven, Sir."

"Okay. Thank you very much. Don't call us. We'll call you … Actually, I was referring to another kind of dish altogether. Lovely boy, don't you think? … Terrific arse."

Robert couldn't contain himself and choked on his Kingfisher beer. "Julian. I can't take you anywhere. You are incorrigible."

Julian made a face and delicately poured his Kingfisher beer into a wine flute.

Bernard leaned forward. "I understand from Robert that you are a stand-up comedian."

Julian sipped beer from his glass. "Yes, one tries to raise a titter or two. I have a regular gig down in Brighton. They do love my Fanny … She's a whippet mongrel. Gorgeous girl. Very much the star of the show."

Robert turned to Magnus. "You must go and see Julian, Magnus. He is rather good. I don't think I've laughed so much in ages."

Julian gave him an affectionate smile. "Thank you, darling. If the cheque bounces, I'll have to pay you in kind." Julian topped up his glass. "I feel compelled to give Robert a bit of a plug here. You see, he really is a modest boy. Did you know that he writes?"

Magnus nodded. "Yes, I did know. But he hasn't really shared anything."

"Robert, you really don't sell yourself enough. If you've got it, flaunt it. That's what I always say. But anyway, he writes the most original farces. Magnus, are you not familiar with the Farndale Avenue Housing Estate Townswomen's Guild Dramatic Society?"

"Can't say I am. It's a bit of a mouthful, isn't it?"

Julian gave him a wide-eyed stare. "Well, you're talking to someone who is a bit of an aficionado when it comes to mouthfuls."

"Julian. Please. I think we need to raise the tone."

Magnus was intrigued. "Have you written many, Robert? They sound interesting."

"I've written a couple. The idea is basically an amateur group butchering classic literature in the worst possible taste, and everything that can go wrong does go wrong. Julian here has been an impressive member of the cast."

Julian smiled. "An impressive member, eh?"

"I'm sorry," said Robert. "He doesn't have an off button."

"Robert's right. I can't stop myself. I'm afraid sexual innuendo is my stock-in-trade."

Bernard laughed. "As we advertising folk like to say, it's your USP."

"I beg your pardon? Is that some kind of sexually transmitted disease?"

They all burst into laughter. "Thankfully, not. Stands for *Unique Selling Proposition*," explained Bernard.

"Unique propositions? I've received a few of those in my time, I can tell you. Anyway, that's enough about me. What's this television commercial that this reprobate is about to star in all about, and is it going to make him obscene piles of money?"

Magnus giggled. "The commercial is for the world's first hand-held computer called the Psion Organiser. And to demonstrate the benefit of being so small we have Robert walking down Gold Hill in Dorset where the famous Hovis commercial was shot, with a fucking big computer system bulging out of his trousers."

Julian lit his first cigarette. "Oh, how lovely. I have just thought of a wonderful line that a second actor might come out with."

Magnus was intrigued. "Well, we weren't planning on having another actor in the commercial, but I'd love to know your thoughts."

"Well, I was thinking that I could enter stage left in a nice little silky number and say those immortal words: 'Is that an entire computer system in your pocket? Or are you just pleased to see me?'"

At this point, the entire table was in hysterics. Julian may have been as smutty as they came, but it was hard not to laugh. Magnus was particularly taken with his ability to latch onto everything that was said and manipulate it in his own inimitable manner. "Bernard, I think we should arrange an agency outing down to Brighton to see this man live."

Julian blew a cloud of cigarette smoke delicately above their heads. "Well, I am flattered, I must say. I will have a word with the manager and arrange front-row seats."

"That is most generous of you, Julian. I'll get my creative secretary to call you, shall I?"

Julian liked this Magnus character. He may not have been his type, but he had a certain kudos. "She can call the theatre and ask to speak to Simon and I shall have a word in Simon's shell-like beforehand. He and I have an understanding, you see. Now, you are very naughty because, like all advertising people I have encountered, you are being economical with the truth."

They all looked a little blank.

"And now you've gone all coy on me. Story of my life. I seem to have this effect on so many attractive men. I have no idea why. Anyway, where was I? Oh yes, you have failed to answer my question regarding Walter Zerlin Junior's remuneration."

Magnus stuttered apologetically. "Well, that is something of a delicate subject that Robert and I need to discuss."

"I do hope he is not being taken advantage of. He is a very talented performer."

Robert was a little embarrassed by Julian's intervention. He knew he had his best interests at heart, but he was desperate to do this commercial as he saw it as a valuable vehicle that would give him the kind of exposure on TV that he needed, and it was completely up his street. The money wasn't the be-all and end-all.

"I can assure you, Julian," added Magnus, "that we always treat our artists with the greatest respect and recognise their talent for which we pay as generously as we can within the constraints of our budget. And a lot will obviously hinge on the success of the campaign. As Robert knows, there will always be an opportunity for the client to buy more media and extend the campaign, which could prove lucrative for Robert."

Julian nodded. "In that case, I shall be sending you my showreel forthwith." As he spoke the waiter returned with a number of metal dishes with their sizzling contents on a trolley. "Oh, I say, the dish of the day has returned."

Chapter 25

Brian sat in the interview room with a polystyrene cup of coffee. Angus was in another room further down the corridor. As he took a sip, a tall balding middle-aged man with a West Country accent and a younger female officer entered the room.

"Good evening, Mr Finkle. I'm Inspector Marks and this is Sergeant Williams. We'd just like to ask you some questions. But before doing so, are you sure that you don't want to have a solicitor present?"

"Thank you, Inspector Marks, but I don't think that will be necessary."

"Very well." Sergeant Williams pressed the record button on the recording device and gesticulated to Inspector Marks. "Today is June 14th 1984. It is 9.45 pm. I am Inspector Marks ID 75962. We are interviewing Brian Finkle, date of birth 22.06.1959. Mr Finkle, can you confirm for the recording that you are aware that the interview is being recorded?" Brian obliged.

"Very good. Mr Finkle, do you also acknowledge that you were previously advised of your constitutional rights and that you signed a statement that detailed those rights and that you agreed to speak to us today without a solicitor?"

"Yes, I acknowledge that."

"Would you like to tell us how you came to discover the body of Mr Bartlett?"

Brian explained that he and Angus had been shooting a TV commercial in the Paddington area with BFCS.

"Out of interest, what is the commercial selling?"

"Simple Soap."

"How interesting. That's one of my wife's favourite brands. She has very sensitive skin, and Simple Soap is the only brand she knows that doesn't contain all that muck that brings her out in a rash. So I suppose you will be using attractive dolly birds."

The young sergeant gave him a disapproving look. "Well, you know what I mean, fashion models."

Brian laughed. He was feeling a little more comfortable now with this old boy. "No, actually we aren't using fashion models; just a white lily. But actually, the lily is a model, another kind of model — a very realistic reproduction of a real lily but about four times the size."

"My goodness. Is that right? It sounds very different to the run-of-the-mill stuff that gets served up these days. Mind you, I do like a few that pop up from time to time. That one in the cinema that is a scene out of *Zulu*, the film about Rorke's Drift. I thought it was going to be some epic film trailer and then this Zulu bloke pops up in the middle of the action selling Silk Cut fags. I always crease up when I see that one. Was it done by Spike Milligan?"

"No, actually it was written by two guys called Paul Weiland and Dave Horry, but I suspect they are big fans of Spike Milligan."

"Oh, and of course there are those real coal fire commercials. They're pretty good, too."

Brian chuckled. "Yeah. They're not bad."

"Anyway, we digress. You say you were shooting this commercial in Paddington. When and why did you decide to travel to Chelsea to visit Mr Bartlett?"

"We wanted to talk to Ben about shooting a commercial because we knew through the grapevine that he was very keen to break into directing commercials and we loved the lighting he employed for his stills photography for which he'd won awards."

"And did he know that you were coming?"

"I know it sounds a bit strange, but we hadn't contacted him. Magnus, our creative director, had used him previously and suggested we just drop in on him after our shoot in Paddington."

"And what time did you arrive?"

"Well, we left the studio in Paddington at about 4.30. Traffic wasn't too bad. It couldn't have taken more than 35 minutes; 40 minutes maybe. So we must have arrived at 10 past or quarter past five."

"And this was in a taxi, was it?"

"Yeah. It was a minicab service used by Brooks Fulford and paid on account. The driver was quite chatty. He'll remember us. The studio and minicab firm will have all the details."

"And how did you gain access to Bartlett's studio?"

Brian explained that they'd found the door open and had entered, discovered the body and phoned the police from a call box from the pub opposite.

Inspector Marks nodded. He had no reason to disbelieve anything Brian had told him. As far as he could tell, Brian was a nice lad who'd stumbled onto a most gruesome and upsetting scene. You could tell instinctively when someone was lying or acting. Brian seemed genuinely in shock in a quiet and subdued way. He even looked pale.

"I'm sorry that you and your colleague have had the misfortune of inadvertently stumbling on the dead body of Mr Bartlett. It's an unsettling thing to do, I know."

"Yeah. You can say that again. I threw up in one of the flower beds outside."

"Oh dear. Well, if it's any consolation, some of us in the force puke up when dealing with murders. Bit of an occupational hazard. And sometimes it can be like a domino effect when other officers puke up on seeing their colleagues puke up. It can get very messy, I can tell you."

Brian suddenly felt a bit queasy. "Oh, I wish you hadn't said that."

"I'm sorry ... Out of interest, what was the commercial you wanted to talk to Bartlett about?"

"Oh, it's for a burglar alarm called *Big Brother*."

"Well, if you need a policeman to appear in it, I'm available, and you won't have to hire any uniforms or a truncheon."

Brian laughed. "Thank you, Inspector. Actually, we are looking to use convicts."

"I beg your pardon?"

"Oh, not real ones, of course. Actors."

"Oh, I see."

"Yeah. The commercial features several men talking about the burglar alarm in negative terms. And then we pull back to reveal that they are all convicts in prison."

Inspector Marks laughed heartily. "That's very good, that is. I do like that. It's a funny thing — I only ever remember the funny commercials on the telly. And that one is right funny. I shall look out for that one."

***

Two rooms along the corridor, Angus was being interviewed by Inspector Haig, an officious spinster in tortoiseshell glasses.

"Mr Lovejoy. This isn't some kind of student common room. Would you please remove your feet from the desk?"

Angus reluctantly obliged. "There's no need to get your knickers in a twist. This is my normal working posture. I get my best ideas sitting in this position, I'll have you know. I think it has something to do with helping the blood flow to the brain."

"Would you please mind your language? You are not at work now, Mr Lovejoy. And I'd remind you that you are here because you have become embroiled in a potential murder enquiry. I need hardly remind you that this is a very serious situation you find yourself in, Mr Lovejoy."

"I always do watch my language. I'm a copywriter, so words matter. I don't have an issue with words like 'knickers' or 'twist', do you?" Inspector Haig blushed and ignored his question. She'd seen his sort before. He was a smart arse. Probably hadn't been properly potty trained as a toddler and hadn't ever respected authority.

Angus had encountered her sort before now. He'd had a teacher at primary school just like her who used to make him do mathematical puzzles on the blackboard, knowing full well that he wouldn't be able to. It was her way of humiliating him in front of the class, and the only way he could hit back was by being an insolent joker. He hadn't changed much in all these years. But he wasn't in the mood for confrontations and just wanted to get this thing done. And he knew the seriousness of his predicament. He didn't need this cow to remind him.

***

Robert had never been very good at holding his drink, and now that he'd consumed three bottles of Kingfisher beer, was beginning to become a little bit more vocal.

"Julian, did I ever tell you about my shoplifting case?"

"Ooh. No, I don't think you have. Do elucidate."

Robert poured himself some water. "I had to defend this young middle-class woman for shoplifting in Marks and Spencer, and one of the witnesses we called was another young lady who was the defendant's flatmate. Anyway, she had been giving evidence that the defendant hadn't been herself that morning. Apparently, she had placed a toilet roll in the fridge. There were some chuckles from the solicitors and the judge intervened. I thought he was going to make some insightful legal observation, but instead, he grinned and said, 'I suppose that would keep it nice and fresh.'"

"Nice to see that humour is alive and well in the courtroom," said Magnus.

"Doesn't happen very often, more's the pity. To be honest, I'd be more than happy to hang up my barrister's wig and do comedy stuff full-time."

"Well, let's hope our TV commercial can help you on your way."

"Thanks, Magnus. I appreciate the opportunity."

Chapter 26

Brian's mother was in the sitting room doing the ironing while her husband sat in an armchair with the *Jewish Chronicle* when the phone rang.

"Hello, Brian. Very nice to hear from you. How are you and Linda? ... What do you mean you are in police custody? ... Maurice, Brian's in police custody."

"What do you mean, he's in police custody?"

"He says he discovered a dead man and the police are asking him questions ... I hope they are feeding you, Brian ... Maurice, he hasn't eaten anything."

"He can't answer questions on an empty stomach."

"Dad says you can't be expected to answer questions on an empty stomach ... He says he's answered all the questions and is just waiting to be released. Well, I hope you get home soon, Brian. Have you told Linda? ... Maurice, he can't get hold of Linda ... You think she's having her hair done? I could always ask Dad to put a note through your door ... Maurice, could you stick a note through his door for Linda?"

"Of course, I can put a note through his door."

"Dad says of course he can put a note through your door. Tell me, do you want me to send over a bowl of chicken soup? ... You'd rather have bean and barley soup and a three-course meal? ... Brian, now isn't the time to make jokes ..."

Chapter 27

"Inspector Goldman. It's Arthur here. I can give you the results of my pathology report. Mr Bartlett's demise was caused by strangulation. The discoid bruises around the neck are very clear to see. You can see exactly where the fingers were placed. There are also fractures to the voice box, fractures to the hyoid bone, as well as petechial haemorrhages — all of which are consistent with neck compression caused by strangulation. The ligature markings to the neck from the rope were made following death. It looks very much as if the body was hung from the neck in the cupboard to make it look like suicide. Time of death would have been approximately 3.00 in the afternoon, at least two hours before it was discovered. So you have a murder enquiry to deal with, Inspector. I hope that's useful."

"Yes, that's very useful, Arthur. Thanks so much for getting back to us so swiftly."

"All part of the service, Inspector. Good day."

Inspector Goldman put the phone down. He wasn't in the least bit surprised. The two lads who'd been interviewed had never been real suspects. By all accounts, they hadn't behaved like suspects. One had been feeling sick and had made a bit of a mess on the floor and the other one had, according to Inspector Haig, been something of a "smart arse". Anyone who'd had the temerity to tell Haig not to get her knickers in a twist had earned his respect, and was unlikely to be someone who'd just committed a murder. He chuckled to himself. They'd had statements now from the film studio, the minicab firm and the pub's landlord. Everything the boys had told them had been corroborated. They could be eliminated from the enquiry. They had a murderer to find.

Chapter 28

"Cyril, darling, can you move that frigging light to my right, and can we try those blue filters?"

The lighting cameraman was no youngster. Unlike Sam the director, who looked as if he hadn't even started to shave yet, this guy directing everyone and everything from behind the camera was obviously the bloke in charge. "I say, Samantha. Would you be a darling and bring Robert's marks another foot back from the camera, please? I want him pin sharp."

Like all commercials, this one enjoyed a fairly sizeable crew. The production company had managed to meet the budget by employing a very junior director and an extremely senior lighting cameraman. It was a clever ploy, as the lighting cameramen of the film industry were the unsung heroes, and would often turn mediocre productions into masterpieces by weaving their special brand of magic. And, of course, they were a lot more affordable than seasoned directors. Dave Watkin was a particularly brilliant lighting man and had worked on several feature films by well-respected film directors including Richard Lester, Peter Brook, Tony Richardson, Mike Nichols, Ken Russell and Hugh Hudson. It just so happened that one of the partners of the production company was a close friend of Watkin, and had managed to persuade the great man to help them out. They'd been particularly fortunate as Watkin, who was usually incredibly busy, was enjoying a lull in his workload.

The location was the same one that Ridley Scott had chosen for his famous Hovis commercial in 1973. Gold Hill, Shaftesbury in Dorset was an incredibly steep cobbled hill. Of course, it had been meant to be a Yorkshire village for the Hovis ad, but once the Yorkshire accented voice-over was laid on top, nobody ever questioned its authenticity. That was the magic of film.

Robert's costume, replete with enormous pockets to accommodate a beautifully constructed computer system made entirely from lightweight polystyrene, was a sight to behold. Robert's comedic skills were at the best of times quite brilliant. He was a natural clown. Now he was in his element.

"Alright. Quiet please on set. Robert, could you come to your marks, please? We'll go for a test run." Dave allowed the director back behind the camera. He was happy and gave Dave the thumbs up and Dave resumed his place behind it. "Okay, camera rolling. And action."

Robert stumbled forward pretending to struggle with his ridiculous load, swaying backwards and forwards down this insane incline like a little sailing boat in a gale force 9. The entire crew including Dave couldn't contain their laughter. It was one of the funniest things they'd ever seen. This unheard-of part-time comedian was some kind of comic genius. "Okay, cut. That was superb, Robert. That was comedy gold on Gold Hill. We'll just watch that back through the video monitor and then we'll go again."

Magnus had missed Robert's run-through. He had been handed a mobile cell phone by the production company's producer. It was the first time he'd been on one of these newfangled phones. It was larger than his desk phone but he could hear Penny as clear as a bell.

"Hi, Magnus. How's it going?"

"Hi, Pen. All's well, thanks. Is everything okay back at the ranch?"

"Well, the good news is that Angus and Brian are now back with us and have been eliminated from police enquiries. I thought I'd better let you know."

"Thanks, hon. Thank Christ for that. I appreciate the call. Are they okay?"

"Yeah. I think so. Angus is back to his usual self and has been raiding your drinks cabinet, but I think Brian was a bit shaken by it to be honest."

"Yeah, I'm not surprised. He's a sensitive lad."

"But have you seen the newspapers?"

"No. Should I have?"

"The police have just made a statement about the death of Benjamin Bartlett. Apparently, he hadn't topped himself. He'd been murdered."

"Shit. You're kidding."

"No. It's been on the radio, too."

"That's terrible. I know it's terrible that he's dead and all that. But murder. That's really ghastly. And who in heaven's name would want to murder Ben? He was a really lovely bloke. Look, will you take the boys out for lunch somewhere nice and put it on my account?"

"Sure. I think I can force myself to go somewhere nice for lunch."

"You're a star, hon."

"Yeah, I know."

"And you can tell the reprobate Lovejoy that if he touches my bottle of Balvenie single malt, he'll be working on the sodding Psion Organiser trade press ad."

***

By the time Magnus returned to the shoot, Robert had completed his first take and spirits seemed very high and several people including Robert were crouching around the video monitor and laughing.

"Hey, Magnus. Where have you been, man?" Dave seemed a little irritated.

"Sorry, Dave. I had to take a call."

"Take a look at this. Can we replay please?"

The video screen went into fast rewind and then sprang back to life. Robert was struggling with his load again and everyone began to laugh spontaneously. Magnus suddenly forgot all about Penny's call and found himself laughing with everyone else. It was contagious. Making funny commercials was a peculiar business. Sometimes you could write something on paper that you thought was funny and then when it was filmed it would leave you cold. And he could never be sure that this script would be funny until Robert got hold of it and showed him how funny it could be. He clapped Robert on the back. "Robert. You really are a funny man. Thanks a million."

"It's my pleasure, Magnus." As an attractive young woman appeared at Robert's side and smiled, Robert gestured towards her. "Oh, let me introduce you to someone, Magnus. This is Melissa. Melissa Bartlett."

***

Magnus could barely believe that Robert and Melissa seemed to be good friends. He had never met her before but knew instantly who she was. Her face was pretty well known and had popped up in the tabloids from time to time, as well as being plastered over poster sites and double-page spreads in the glossies. He didn't mention Ben's murder, of course. It just seemed inappropriate and would have cast a shadow over an otherwise enjoyable day. There was nothing wrong with the two of them being close or having a liaison. She was in the process of divorcing Ben, after all. But it just felt a bit odd coming on the heels of her husband's very sudden and grisly demise.

At the end of the day's filming, he waved goodbye to Robert as he stepped into Melissa's open-top Porsche and chatted at length with Dave Watkin, who was an interesting man with lots of anecdotes to tell. But now he was tired and was going to turn in early. It was a two-day shoot, and more than half of the set-ups were already in the can. In the past, he'd often stayed up late with the crew, drinking and socialising into the wee small hours. But these days, he didn't have the stamina or appetite for it. And besides, Robert the man of the hour had buggered off with his surprise girlfriend. Had he still been around, he might have been tempted. Robert was a lovely man and made him laugh, and Magnus was convinced that his friend would indeed end up hanging up his barrister's wig and making a name for himself in the entertainment world. It was just a matter of time. And when that happened, Magnus would be the first to remind him that he'd been one of those who'd helped him on his way.

Chapter 29

"Hello. Reverend Chapman speaking."

"Robin, dear man. How are you? It's Roy here."

"Well thanks, Roy. But I can't help thinking about poor Ben. To be honest, it hasn't really sunk in."

"I know. It's a ghastly business. And I can't get used to the idea of him not being around. It's horrible. And that's partly why I thought I'd call, Robin. You see, I'm thinking about arranging a memorial service for him in a couple of weeks."

"That's a lovely idea, Roy."

"As you know, Ben was actually quite spiritual and religious in his own way and was known to attend church services. In fact, Melissa, his wife, has just called me to say that he stipulated in his will that he wanted to be cremated and have his ashes spread on the cricket pitch at the Hurlingham Club." At this point, Roy's tearful voice faltered and he took a few moments to recover his composure. "Anyway, I thought we could arrange to have a memorial service at the Hurlingham Club. We can hire one of the rooms and you, being a man of the cloth, might like to officiate."

There was a hesitation at the other end of the line.

"I hope you don't mind me asking, Robin."

"No, not at all. It's just that something has cropped up with Samantha's mother, and I've agreed at the last minute to take time off to go with her to Hamburg."

"Oh, heavens. Is she alright?"

"Well, we don't really know. We think she's had some kind of stroke. Anyway, we'll find out more when we get there. And we'll probably have to move her to a care home."

"I'm sorry to hear that, Robin. Do send my very best wishes to Samantha. When are you flying out?"

"Well, that's the thing … We're flying off tomorrow morning at sparrow's fart, and I'm likely to be gone for some while, as we have the apartment there. Of course, I'd have stepped in had this not been the case, but as it happens, there is someone I could certainly recommend if you're looking for a God bod."

Roy laughed. "How nicely put. Well, yes that would be appreciated, Robin."

"His name's Simon Granger. He's the vicar of St Peter's Hammersmith. Terribly nice chap. Samantha is an old friend of his wife; that's how we got to know each other. I'm sure he'd be only too pleased to step in. Oh, and get this, he's rather a keen cricketer. You could even ask him if he'd like a game. He's a bit of an all-rounder apparently and opened the innings for his university."

"We'd be killing two birds with one stone."

"And here's a thought, Roy: you could even follow the memorial service with a memorial match. I think Ben would have liked that."

"I think you're right, Robin. Why on earth didn't I think of that? What a fabulous idea."

"It's such a shame I won't be here. I would love to have been with you for that."

"You'll be with us in spirit, Robin. I can assure you that you will most definitely be with us in spirit."

Chapter 30

It was barely daybreak. Chaz had never been on the allotment before at such an unearthly hour, but he didn't want to be spotted. He let himself through the rickety iron gates with his keys and relocked them behind him. As he made his way past the community hut and greenhouses, a crow protested and swooped overhead. His plot was over at the far side, adjacent to a small cemetery. Only the dead could see him now as he removed the package from his rucksack. He'd stuffed everything into the paper bag: latex gloves, trousers, shirt, jumper, shoes, underwear, the lot. You couldn't be too careful. Then he recovered the box of matches and firelighters from his tumbledown shed.

The bag lit easily enough but once he added the firelighters, the flames really took hold and bathed the nearby raspberry canes and apple trees in its luminous orange glow. In no time at all, the contents had been incinerated to grey ash. He breathed a deep sigh of relief. The deed had been done. The evidence had been destroyed. He could live again.

Chapter 31

"Take a pew, chaps. I'll be with you shortly. Nature calls, I'm afraid."

Angus and Brian slumped into Magnus's leather sofa and listened to his new Denon hi-fi system that he'd switched on to Radio Four's lunchtime news, broadcasting live from the House of Commons where Dr David Owen was asking Secretary of State Leon Brittan if he was going to make a statement over the measures the government intended taking to prevent a repeat of the violence and public disorder that had occurred at the Orgreave coking plant in South Yorkshire the previous day in connection with the miners' industrial dispute. In response, Leon Brittan said that 10,000 people had attended to help stop British Steel from exercising its lawful right to remove coke from the plant, and that the police were subjected to a considerable level of violence that necessitated the use of mounted officers and officers equipped with riot shields and helmets. Apparently, 93 people were arrested of whom 26 had been charged with unlawful assembly, assault and public order offences. And 28 police officers suffered injuries.

"In spite of the large numbers of people present and the violence which arose, the police were able to ensure that the vehicles due to go into and out of the plant were able to do so as required," said Brittan. "What there is need for now," he continued, "is unequivocal and unanimous condemnation of the use of violence as a means of securing political or industrial objectives; and full support for those who are determined to ensure that violence shall not prevail." This was greeted with the sounds of unanimous vocal approval from the government's own benches.

Magnus returned. "Christ. I've heard enough about this sodding miners' strike. I can't see British Coal stumping up for another TV campaign for real coal fires next year the way things are going." He closed the door and switched off the tuner. "It's been a bit of a manic week."

"One way of putting it," said Angus. "Two commercials and one murder. And it wasn't even a bloody account man who got topped. That poor bloke, though ..."

Magnus poured coffee. "Yeah. It's bloody awful. He was a lovely man. I can't begin to imagine why anyone would want to kill him. And it couldn't have been much fun for you two discovering the poor sod and then getting held for questioning for 24 bleeding hours."

Brian sipped at his coffee. "I've been getting nightmares ever since. But the police were perfectly nice. They were just doing their job. Funnily enough, the policeman who interviewed me was a lovely old boy. Turns out his wife is a big fan of Simple Soap, and he loved the sound of our Big Brother commercial. Even said he'd be available if we wanted to use a policeman in the commercial."

"I suppose he could probably point us in the direction of a few criminals," quipped Angus.

"Nice idea, Shaggers," added Magnus. "We could have a casting in the form of an identity parade."

"Why didn't I think of that one?"

"You usually do ... Anyway, to return to work, I'll show you mine if you show me yours."

"Last time I had this kind of exchange was in the school playground," said Angus. "If memory serves me right, her name was Deborah."

"Alright, alright. Save us the details, Shaggers. I'll kick off, shall I?" Magnus pulled himself out of his swivel chair and rifled through his detritus on the shelves, and picked out a U-matic, which he thrust into his video player. "It hasn't been graded, but otherwise, it's virtually there. But before I play it, I just want to tell you a funny story about Roy Plomley."

"We're all ears."

"He's a lovely old buffer. Very charming and everything you'd expect. He did one take, which was perfect. And we did one more just to be on the safe side. He was in the studio for no more than five minutes and we had a nice chat about *Desert Island Discs* over a cup of tea and biscuits. And then, just before leaving to go home, he turned to me and said quite earnestly, 'Would you like me to do a hard-sell version?' And I stupidly said, 'No, that's fine Roy.' But I wish I'd said, 'Yes, please.' The idea of Roy Plomley doing a hard-sell voice-over would have been quite something, don't you think?"

"Do you think it would have been any different?" asked Brian.

"It's a good point, Brian. I suppose the difference in his delivery would probably have been minimal. But we'll never know. Anyway, here's the ungraded version. See what you think." Magnus drew the blinds and switched on the video player. The steep hill in Dorset filled the screen. It was beautifully lit to look like early morning or dusk and the figure of Robert struggling with an entire computer system bulging from his trousers came stumbling into view. It was pure, unadulterated comedy straight out of Laurel and Hardy's *The Piano*. As Robert did his thing, Roy's dulcet, lugubrious tones complemented the visuals beautifully. "Imagine carrying around an entire computer system in your pocket. Now, thanks to the Psion Organiser, you can — without looking like a prize plonker.

"The Psion Organiser. The world's first pocket-sized computer. At just £90, it really is light on your pocket."

Magnus turned off the machine and turned to Angus and Brian who were both grinning like Cheshire cats. "As my folks would say, mazel tov, Magnus."

"Thanks, Brian."

"Your Robert guy is a good egg, isn't he?" added Angus. "And how the hell did you get it to look so beautiful with that director who's been directing commercials for all of two minutes?"

"We got a bit lucky, to be honest. The production company had to keep costs down, so they used their most junior director and teamed him up with one of the best lighting cameramen in the business. It was a very clever move, because the lighting guy basically directed while the director got to learn a lot from this guy in the process. And at the end of the day, we've come away with a classy bit of film."

"What's this cameraman's name?" asked Brian.

"Nice man called Dave Watkin. He's been the lighting cameraman on a number of big films including *Chariots of Fire*."

"Blimey! No wonder it looks so bloody good."

"Yeah, I know. Frankly, we were incredibly lucky to get Watkin. He's normally far too busy and doesn't usually go anywhere near commercials. But Frank Milner, who's a partner at the production company, is a good mate and somehow managed to swing it. Now, to change the subject, how's your production going?"

Brian opened a large brown envelope that he had in his hand and pulled out a video. "This is the rough cut with voice. We've seen it so many times in dark studios that we're sick of seeing the bloody thing."

Magnus knew the feeling. It was mind-boggling how many hours went into honing a 30-second film, not to mention the number of people involved in producing it. It was actually totally insane.

Brian shoved the large plastic brick into the U-matic machine and the white lily filled the screen and was duly sprayed with perfume and paint by elegant robotic arms while the voice of Joanna Lumley narrated throughout.

Even though it hadn't been graded and the music hadn't yet been scored, you could see that it was a classy production that delivered a fairly powerful and emotive message.

Magnus switched off the monitor. "It's exactly as I imagined it. Very stylish and very powerful. Well done, boys. I think we should add the music before revealing it to the client. Len has done you proud. But then, he's a real pro. Very good choice of voice, too."

"We had to ask Joanna Lumley to read the script quite a few times, though," said Angus.

"Really?"

"Yeah. It's funny. She automatically went into her sultry advertising voice, and we had to keep telling her that we wanted her normal everyday voice. I think she thought we were a bit mad at first. But her normal speaking voice is so lovely and appropriate. Anyway, we got there in the end. And she was absolutely charming."

Magnus nodded. "Well done, lads. A sultry voice would have killed the idea completely. It's a bloody powerful commercial and I suspect it's going to sell shed loads of product."

Angus and Brian instinctively rose from the sofa and headed for the door.

Magnus stopped them. "Actually, there's one other thing I was going to say." He closed the door as Brian and Angus sat down again. "It's just something I felt a bit disconcerted about. Don't worry, it's nothing to do with you. When I was on the set down in Dorset, Robert introduced me to a friend who turned out to be none other than Melissa Bartlett."

Angus raised his eyebrows. "She hasn't wasted any time, then. While her husband's in the freezer drawer she's been turning up the heat on her love life with a spicy little takeaway."

"How very delicately put, Angus. But yes, it's all a bit unseemly. But having said that, is it? Is it really? I mean, she was in the process of divorcing him, after all."

"Why don't you tell Magnus about Bartlett's life assurance?" said Brian.

"Life assurance?" asked Magnus.

"Yeah," replied Angus. "Let's just say I did a little bit of digging. He had life assurance alright, and I suspect he took it out when insuring his equipment, which will be insured for a fairly tidy sum. A mate of mine told me a while back that most photographers he knows have life policies that are worth millions. Melissa would be a very rich lady with her husband six feet under."

Magnus grimaced. "Nah. I don't buy it. She's already loaded. She doesn't need the money. And the way Ben talked, they were on reasonable terms. They were still friends. He may have had a sizeable life policy, but I don't think it would be of any interest to his wife."

Chapter 32

"Is that Mrs Melissa Bartlett?"

"Yes. Speaking."

"Mrs Bartlett, on behalf of the Equitable Life, may I firstly extend my sincerest condolences? The news of the passing of your dear beloved husband came as a very great shock to us."

"Thank you, Mr ..."

"It's Alexander Mellows speaking."

"Well, thank you, Mr Mellows. It has been a very difficult time. Despite our imminent divorce, my husband and I were still good friends, and I still had feelings for him. He was a decent man, Mr Mellows. And nobody on God's earth deserves to be brutally murdered."

"Quite ... I hope you don't think me indelicate, but I wanted to call you as you're the named beneficiary on your late husband's life policy."

"Oh yes, one of your salesmen called me some days ago and I called back."

"Really? What was this concerning, Mrs Bartlett?"

"Something to do with Ben wanting to raise his premiums."

"Let me have a look in his file. One moment, Mrs Bartlett." There was a clunk as the receiver was put down and Melissa could hear papers being frantically shuffled around. This went on for some minutes. And then the receiver sprang to life again. "How very strange, Mrs Bartlett. There are no notes in his file to suggest that anyone had spoken to your late husband about this matter. And his premiums were already on the high side."

"Yes, I thought as much. I couldn't understand why he'd want to raise them. He knew that I wouldn't need the money."

"Did the salesman you spoke to leave a name, Mrs Bartlett?"

"Yes, he did ... What was it now? Oh yes, that's right. His surname was Manilow, like the singer. Angus Manilow."

"Are you sure, Mrs Bartlett?"

"Well, of course, I'm sure. I never forget a name."

"Well, that is most peculiar because we don't employ anyone by that name here. I have a list of our employees in front of me and there is not one single person by the name of Manilow working for us. The call you received must have been from a fraudster. I suggest you report it to the police."

"Oh, dear. The last thing I want to do is talk to them again. It feels like I've been spending the best part of my life speaking to that lot. Is there anything else you wanted to say, Mr Mellows?"

"Well yes, I wanted to say that your late husband did have a very sizeable life policy in place, which we will, of course, honour as soon as we receive the death certificate. We take a great deal of pride, Mrs Bartlett, in the timely manner in which we settle life policies. We see it as our duty to the bereaved. It may seem like a small detail, but for us, it is terribly important, and I just wanted to reassure you, Mrs Bartlett, that we will do our utmost to ensure that funds are paid swiftly into your account. In most cases within five days of receiving said death certificate."

"Thank you for that reassurance, Mr Mellows. It is comforting to know that. I have always been a big fan of the Equitable Life. You seem like a very fair company when it comes to commission. You see, I do follow the financial press, which has looked on your company most favourably in this respect."

"Thank you, Mrs Bartlett. It has always been our policy to be transparent about our fees, which as you rightly say, are the lowest in the market and always upfront."

"Oh, and out of interest, can you tell me how much my late husband's life was insured for?"

"Indeed I can, Mrs Bartlett. His life was insured with us for five and a half million pounds."

"My goodness. That's a lot of money."

"It certainly is, Mrs Bartlett."

***

"Ah, chaps. How are we doing? Have you got over your ordeal with the police? I was really sorry you had to go through all that." Bernard was wearing jeans and a chunky cardigan and for a split second, Brian didn't recognise him.

"We're fine, thanks. All behind us now. Are you turning into a creative or something, Bernard?"

"Don't worry. Your jobs are safe. I won't be moving down here to compete with you ... No. I've decided that I'm only going to wear the suit when I have client meetings. To be perfectly honest, I can't abide wearing a bloody suit and tie. It physically restrains you in all kinds of ways, so this will be my sartorial look for a good deal of the time. The suit is going to live on the back of my door hanging in a suit bag."

Angus finished writing copy for a press ad for Warres port and looked up from his pad. "Did I hear you say that you're going to become as scruffy as the smelly creatives?"

"Basically. Yes."

"Excellent. I always saw you as a bit of a scruffy bastard. Nice bit of schmatta, don't you think, Finklebum?"

"Yeah, very nice schmatta."

"I'll have you know that I paid good money for this schmatta at Harvey Nicks. By the way, massive congratulations. Magnus has just unveiled your masterpiece for Simple Soap. I knew it was going to be good. But it blew me away. And I love the way Len gets the spray gun to point at us the viewers when Joanna Lumley asks: 'Would you add artificial colouring?' That's a brilliant piece of directing."

"Yeah, that was Len's idea. It really works, doesn't it?"

"Not half. It's those brilliant little touches that make something like this so powerful. I'm going to suggest we present it to the clients here tomorrow if that's okay with you. I think you'd better brace yourself for another one of Keith's squidgy kisses. I'll let you know what time we're on as soon as I get confirmation from them. Now, the other reason I came down was to put another little brief your way. It's for a new piece of business — a chocolate bar called Spira from Cadbury's. Now, I know you are juggling all kinds of things at the mo, so feel free to tell me to fuck off. I won't take it personally. John and Shena are already working on it and Magnus will be having a crack at it, too."

Angus assumed his thinking position with his feet on the desk and a pen behind the right ear. "What do you reckon, Bry?"

"Fine by me. I'm up for a bit more juggling. Sounds like it might be interesting."

"Okay. That's great. I'm not actually working on this business. It's being given to the new boy. And I'm just overseeing it."

"New boy?" asked Brian. "I didn't know we'd hired another suit."

Magnus closed the door. "Yes. He hasn't been introduced yet. His name's Douglas Selby. Slightly odd bloke if you want my honest opinion. Collects bus tickets and timetables. And he got himself onto Mastermind last year. His specialist subject was the Routefinder bus, 1945 to 1959. Shall I tell him to brief you this afternoon?"

Angus made a face. "Oh, I don't know. Do we have to? He doesn't sound like the full ticket."

"I suppose we can always get off at the next stop."

"Shall I point him in your direction then?"

Angus nodded. "Go on then. I'll get the straightjacket out just in case he has a funny turn."

***

"Angus, I know I should be feeling pretty good about everything at the moment, but I can't stop thinking about that poor sod Bartlett. Keeps bloody haunting me. I mean, everything else is ..."

"Bloody insignificant ... Those are the words I think you're looking for," added Angus.

"Yeah. This stuff is only bloody advertising fluff."

"We work in a pretty shallow world, you and me, Brian. But as shallow worlds go, it isn't half bad. But I know what you mean. Look, I know I can seem a bit callous and uncaring at times, but actually, that whole thing with Bartlett has affected me, too. I didn't want to say anything, but I've been having problems sleeping at night. And Sam wants me to go to see someone about it. She knows a psychotherapist in St John's Wood, and I kind of pooh-poohed the idea. But perhaps she's right. Maybe I should talk to this dude. Maybe we both should."

Brian nodded. "Yeah. You might be right. Linda said something similar."

"Talking of this industry being shallow. I was thinking the other day about the plethora of crap commercials that grace our screens. Do you think other creative teams actually set out to write the kind of facile stuff that so often ends up on the box or do you think they start out with half-decent ideas that just get watered down and turned into junk?"

Brian shrugged. "I haven't really thought about it. Perhaps a mixture of both."

"Strange isn't it, to think that some people get hired to write that kind of stuff? I mean, if we were expected to churn that out it would be bloody easy, but you wouldn't receive any kind of job satisfaction, would you?"

Brian nodded. "It would be bloody embarrassing. Someone might ask you at a dinner party what you did. And you'd have to say I write all those bloody awful commercials for something like Pedigree Chum."

"It would be so bloody easy though." Angus picked up his portable typewriter and placed a piece of A4 paper beneath the ribbon and rolled the paper to the top of the page. "And to prove it, time me."

Brian laughed. "What are you doing, Shaggers?"

"I'm writing a crap commercial for this Spira chocolate bar. So time me."

"You're mad. But okay, I'm timing you."

Angus started to bash away at his typewriter while Brian looked through a photographer's book. It never ceased to amaze him how incredibly elaborate photographers' portfolios were. Invariably, they'd have large leather covers with their name or logo embossed at huge expense into the hide and high-quality prints would be mounted and professionally bound into the book. In most instances, the book itself would slide out of a large leather slipcase. To stand a reasonable chance of getting seen by a fair number of art directors, photographers would have to assemble a fair number of books to circulate. You'd need a mortgage to pay for it all. It was little wonder that they charged so much.

"Okay. Stop the watch. How long was that?"

Brian looked at his watch. "That was pretty quick. Four and a half minutes."

Angus rolled out the piece of paper and handed it to Brian. "There you go. One crappy 30-second TV commercial in four and a half minutes. Take a look at that and tell me it's a load of crap."

Brian read it and laughed. "That's a load of crap alright."

Angus had written a spoof commercial that had an elderly couple sitting in a cinema admiring an inane commercial on the big screen that showed a revolving chocolate bar with all its constituent ingredients in their full glory.

"I suppose if you became accustomed to churning out stuff like that you'd end up spending more time in the pub. So there is a silver lining of sorts. Talking of which, why don't we get out of here and continue this conversation down the road?"

Brian smiled. "You want to drink already?"

"No, not beer. I found this amazing place in Litchfield Street yesterday. It's called Bunjies and it's run by this extraordinary little guy who chain smokes and wears a cravat. He serves coffee and great grub, but the main reason to go there is to chat with him. He runs the place like a club, and if he likes you, he doesn't even let you pay."

"You're kidding."

"No, I'm not. I had to argue with him. So I just left money on the bar, and he wasn't happy, I can tell you. But the thing is, he's a real character with loads of anecdotes and an amusing turn of phrase. I think you'll love him. And I have a sneaking suspicion that he's one of your lot."

"Oh right. He's a little Jewish fella, is he? Well, if he's small and funny, that's almost a certainty. What's his name?"

"Lou. Lou Hart. Come on, get your jacket on, Finklebrain. I'll introduce you."

***

Douglas Selby was ambitious and had a reasonably high opinion of himself. He'd acquired a First Class Honours degree from Queen's College, Cambridge in Mechanical Engineering and had spent a few years at Saatchi & Saatchi on the Cadbury's account. Now he'd landed a position at the creative hot shop, Gordon Deedes Rutter, and he was raring to go.

When he stepped into Angus and Brian's office at the allotted time, he was surprised and mildly annoyed that they weren't there. He took a seat on their sofa and twiddled his thumbs. This place was a bit too laid back for his liking. He was used to getting things done and taking charge. He flicked open the smart folio of photographs that lay on the table. They didn't do much for him. A bit too arty for his liking. He had simple tastes. Their shelves were filled with art books, D&AD Annuals and novels by Tom Sharpe. On the wall over Angus's desk were a series of bold quotations. One read: *I don't want to achieve immortality through my work; I want to achieve immortality through not dying.*

I don't want to live on in the hearts of my countrymen; I want to live on in my apartment. Underneath in smaller type was the name Woody Allen. There was another large black and white print of an ad for the Volkswagen Beetle. But there was no car in sight. Instead, there was a large unflattering portrait of the comedian Marty Feldman with bulbous eyes, and the headline read: *If he can make it, so can Volkswagen.* It wasn't the kind of ad he really subscribed to. He knew it was for the Beetle but your average punter wouldn't without reading the copy, and there had been countless studies about the amount of time the average person spent looking at a press ad. The vast majority didn't read body copy. Okay, it was mildly amusing in a self-deprecating kind of way, but that alone wouldn't sell VW Beetles.

Where were these two clowns? He knew that they were treated with a great deal of respect. There couldn't have been many creative teams that had bagged a D&AD Silver at such an early stage in their careers. The reminder sat on Brian's shelf in the form of a modest but unmistakable D&AD pencil. That six-inch piece of wood had no doubt hiked up their salaries hugely. And they could presumably now work at any agency that took their fancy. But that alone didn't excuse them from standing him up like this. It was bad form. He was beginning to consider whether to sit here any longer when his eyes fell upon that single piece of A4 paper that lay on Angus's desk next to his telephone. He picked it up. It was a TV script for the Spira chocolate bar. How extraordinary. They had already written the script before receiving the brief from him.

He read it through carefully. It was perfect. It highlighted all the product attributes, showed the chocolate bar in extreme close-up, and even included a giant logo. It was the kind of commercial he approved of. It was totally relevant and very easy to sell. He took the script and photocopied it on the photocopier in the corridor, and then placed the original back on Angus's desk. His annoyance with Angus and Brian had dissipated. He wasn't going to hang about. He'd get the ball rolling and show initiative.

He knew that he'd be able to sell this easily, which would give the agency plenty of time for pre-production. This was his big opportunity to make his mark; take a lead; and get noticed. His gung-ho attitude had served him well at Saatchi & Saatchi. Now it was time to shake this place up a bit. Show them how it's really done. All he had to do was transfer the script onto headed paper and call the client. *Play your cards right,* he thought to himself, *and come Christmas, a nice fat bonus will be winging its way to you.*

Chapter 33

Bunjies was a curious place. Brian wouldn't have given it a second glance. As you entered, there were a couple of tables and a counter with a girl serving coffee and snacks and in the far corner, narrow spiral stairs took you down into a cavernous world of dank, whitewashed arches and a series of tables and chairs. Presiding over one of them was a diminutive, fairly dapper man with slicked-back, Brylcreemed hair, cravat and navy blazer. There were a couple of old boys with him hanging on his every word. Angus gesticulated at Lou who immediately acknowledged him.

"Angus. Pull up a chair and join us. Allow me to introduce you to Stephen and George."

"Very nice to meet you. And this is my partner in crime, Brian." Brian stepped out of the shadows and took a seat.

"It's very nice to meet you, Brian. I was just telling Stephen and George about this place and how I came to own it."

Stephen picked up a bottle of wine and offered it to Brian and Angus. "It's very good by the way. Château d'Angludet 1974."

"So how did you come to own this place, Lou?" asked Brian.

"I was very fortunate, Brian. I wasn't academic and did badly at school. I was a right lobbus."

Angus looked perplexed. "Lobbus?"

Lou laughed. "Forgive me. I'm slipping into Yiddish parlance."

"Lobbus," explained Brian, "is a rascal."

Angus nodded. "I thought I'd bring my interpreter."

Lou smiled. "And you know what we call people like you, Angus?"

Angus shrugged. "Enlighten me."

"A meshuggener."

Brian laughed. "It means a crazy person."

"If it's any consolation, Angus," added Lou, "I too am a meshuggener. I think the best people on this planet usually are. Anyway, to get back to your question, Brian, after the war, having been the shortest man to serve in the Eighth Army in Africa, I did a string of dead-end jobs."

"Were you really the shortest?" asked Angus.

Lou looked at Angus as if he was a complete fool. "Well, put it this way, if you should ever meet another bloke shorter than me who served in the Eighth Army, I'd love to meet him. As a matter of fact, and this is a true story, they couldn't even issue me with official desert boots. My feet were too small. They simply didn't have them in my size. So I must have been the only member of the esteemed Eighth Army to serve his country in brown brogues."

They all laughed as Lou took a sip from his wine glass. Then he reached into his jacket pocket, removed a leather wallet and pulled out an old piece of paper, which he then carefully unfolded. "The story isn't apocryphal. Here's the evidence, M'lord." He handed the piece of browning paper to Angus who held it out for all of them to see.

Pte. L Hart, RAOC, Brown Brogues, permission for the use of.
This is my authority for Pte Hart to wear while on active service brown brogues, size boys' 7, until suitable boots are requisitioned or made or this permission is revoked.

Commanding Officer,
First Light Repair Section RAOC
August 15th 1942

The signature was an illegible squiggle.

"That's incredible," said Brian. "And you have kept this all those years." Angus returned the evidence to Lou.

"Well, wouldn't you have — had you been in my shoes? Anyway, after the war, things were far less interesting. I took a string of dead-end jobs. But then, thank God, on 29 January 1949, I got lucky." He lit a cigarette and placed it in a cigarette holder and took a long drag. They all watched him intently and said nothing. "Because on 29 January 1949, I received a letter. Brown manilla envelope addressed to me. Looked like nothing special. Anyway, I opened it and nearly had a heart attack." He took a sip of wine. "Because inside the envelope was a short letter from Vernons Football Pools. I'd won £5,000. These days, that doesn't sound like such a large sum but back then, that was a lot of money. So I thought I'd set myself up in business. I bought two sweet shops, which did quite well. I eventually sold them and bought this place. Funny thing was that I thought I was just buying a café with a cellar attached. Turns out I actually bought a live music venue with a coffee bar attached. This tiny cellar became the hottest live music venue during the 60s. You wouldn't believe it, would you?"

"There's hardly enough room to swing a cat down here," said Angus.

Lou looked at him. "Talking of cats. We had our very own swinging cat down here. He was a pretty cool cat. Do you know what his name was? I'll tell you. His name was Cat Stevens."

"No. Really? Are you serious?" asked Angus.

"Of course. He used to do the washing up here. Then one Wednesday evening he played live. Nobody knew he was a musician. They all came to Bunjies in the 60s. Al Stewart, Sandie Shaw, Paul Simon, Art Garfunkle, David Bowie. You name them, they came. And then in 1964, this meshuggener with sunglasses turns up one evening and doesn't seem to want to pay. So I insist that he has to pay like anyone else and one of his friends pays for him. And then towards the end of the session, he borrows a guitar and starts to play. His name was Bob Dylan."

Brian was well impressed. "*The* Bob Dylan?"

Lou smiled. "Like I say. The best people are meshuggeners."

"See. I told you, Brian," said Angus. "This man has some incredible stories."

"We all collect stories, don't we?" said Lou. "And you have had to contend with that pretty grim murder story."

"Yeah. I've been having nightmares about that poor sod Benjamin Bartlett," replied Brian.

"Benjamin Bartlett? Are you sure that that was his name?" asked Lou.

"Yeah. Why?"

Lou bit his lip and wracked his brain. "I've had a bloke in here for coffee several times and about a fortnight ago we had a bit of a chat and he asked me if I'd seen someone, and I'm pretty sure he said the guy that he was looking for was named Ben Bartlett. I'd completely forgotten about it. Do you think he could have been the murderer?"

"Christ! That's possible. Did he leave a name?" asked Brian.

"No, he didn't. But I'm pretty sure he wasn't a policeman or private detective."

"And do you remember what he looked like?" asked Angus.

"Yeah. Funnily enough, he looked a bit like Bob Dylan. But I'm sure he couldn't sing."

"Nor can Bob Dylan," added Angus.

They all laughed except Lou.

"Maybe I should go to the police. Yes, I think I'll do that," he said to himself. And stubbed out his cigarette.

Chapter 34

He'd taken clients here before. He liked the place. It was close by and the food was fabulous. Back in 1921, The Wolseley had been a very swish car showroom for the Wolseley motorcar. Today it was a very swish restaurant for executives with healthy expense accounts.

"Good afternoon, Sir. Would you like to order a drink?"

Douglas raised his hand. "No, thank you. I'll wait for my two guests to arrive first."

As he took a look at the menu, his two guests were shown to the table.

"Douglas. It's good to see you. This is Caroline." The tall silver-haired executive shook Douglas by the hand as did his younger female sidekick. "I'm very impressed that you got back to us so incredibly quickly. Most agencies take a minimum of two weeks. I don't think you had the brief for two days."

Douglas laughed. "Yeah, well we like to get things moving swiftly at GDR, Dan. I thought I'd just show you our idea before we look at the menu, and you can digest it so to speak and give me your initial feedback."

"Okay. Sounds good to me." Caroline nodded enthusiastically as Dan slipped his reading glasses on and looked at the wine menu. "Wouldn't say no to a glass of the Chardonnay if that's alright."

"Of course." Douglas gesticulated to the waiter who came straight to the table.

"We'll have a bottle of Chardonnay, please, and a large jug of water. And Caroline, would you like something?"

"Thank you, Douglas. I'll have a G & T if I may." The waiter bowed and disappeared.

Douglas reached below the table and took two scripts from his attaché case and placed them in front of his guests. They took a couple of minutes to read the scripts. Dan spoke first.

"Well, first of all, thank you for this super speedy response. I don't think I have any issues with this script, Douglas. It seems to tick all the boxes. And I just love this bit here," he laughed.

"What's that?" asked Douglas.

"Sorry. It's the logo at the end that fills the entire screen. And I laugh because we have just had something of a row with one of our other agencies over the size of the logo. We just wanted to enlarge it a little bit and they went ballistic. And here you are suggesting that we fill the entire screen with the logo. I don't think I've ever seen that done before. It's pretty radical." He turned to his colleague. "What do you think, Caroline?"

"I think it's very direct and to the point. The messaging is spot on. And we get to see the product nice and big, too. I don't think anyone will have a problem with this. It isn't the least bit contentious. I wouldn't bother researching it either, Dan. It's very refreshing to see something so straightforward and uncluttered by some hifalutin idea."

"Well, there we have it, Douglas. Excellent work. It looks like we have a TV commercial to produce. Caroline and I will present it to the rest of the team. I think Caroline is right. I can't see anyone on the board objecting to this, and she may be right about research, too. Can I leave that one with you to propose, Caroline? It will save a fair bit of money."

Douglas was feeling elated. He'd only gone and bloody sold his first commercial for Gordon Deedes Rutter, and nobody back in Great Pulteney Street had a clue that he was here. He couldn't wait to tell Bernard and see the surprise on his face.

Chapter 35

He always reserved Wednesday afternoons for visiting his parishioners who needed comforting; those who were mourning the loss of a loved one; or had become traumatised by some other seismic event; or those who were simply lonely and elderly.

Raymond Blunt fell into the last category. He wasn't entirely lonely in the strict sense of the word. His wife still lived with him but was now in the early stages of Parkinson's disease. She may have still had her faculties but conversations were generally speaking of the one-way variety. This, however, did not deter Raymond from engaging in normal conversations with his wife for whom he would usually answer. There were times, of course, when she would talk and smile in response to his voice. And these responses, though small, were heartening and made her husband feel that his efforts were not in vain.

Reverend Granger had known Raymond longer than most in the congregation and the two men had grown close. They had much in common. They had both studied Divinity at the University of St Andrews, Scotland's most historic seat of learning, and while Granger had chosen to take the path to the church, Blunt had taken a far more circuitous path through life that included the army, the law, and education. The two also shared a passion for literature, cinema and the sacred music of William Byrd — particularly his masses and the sublime Ave verum corpus. Despite the fact that Blunt was at least 25 years his senior, his views and outlook on life were anything but entrenched and conservative. While he didn't subscribe to party politics, he expressed liberal and fairly progressive views on most subjects and Granger felt that he could talk freely about his sexuality and the inevitable conflicts this created within certain areas of the church and his spiritual life. Blunt wasn't gay but was very close to his gay son and could relate to Granger's dilemmas and internal conflicts.

As Reverend Granger tapped on the door, his good friend opened it.

"Ah, Simon. I saw you coming up the path. What a glorious day it is."

"All the more glorious for seeing you, Raymond. How are things?"

"Oh, you know. One gets by as best as one can. Susan is sleeping, so we should probably retreat to the study otherwise we may disturb her."

They climbed the old stairs and parked themselves in a study that was lined wall to ceiling with books. Raymond opened a cabinet and produced a bottle of whisky and two tumblers and poured two generous glasses, handing one to his friend.

"Thank you, Raymond. That's very kind. So how have you been?"

"Well, thanks. Do you know, Susan and I had a grand day out yesterday. I took her to the cinema. No ordinary cinema — the oldest cinema in London."

"How wonderful. Is that the Phoenix?"

"No, it's the Regent Street Cinema. It's funny — all these years I've lived in London and have never discovered it before now. You must go, Simon. It's a gem of a place and still retains a few original features. It screened its first movie back in 1896, would you believe."

"My word. I must make a note to make a visit. What did you see?"

"*Local Hero.*"

"Oh yes. I've heard good things about it."

"It's a wonderful film. You'd like it, Simon. It's all about this American oil executive who is sent to a remote Scottish island to buy up a whole village to make way for an oil refinery. I won't say anything more. I wouldn't want to spoil it for you. But it's funny and strangely touching. And do you know something? ... Even Susan smiled. So it must have been a bit special."

"Now, haven't I read something about the writer and director in *The Times*?"

"Yes. You have. I read that article, too. His name is Bill Forsyth and he was a teacher."

"That's right. And didn't he put a load of kids from his class into his films?"

"Indeed. His first film was made on a shoestring and used teenagers from the community centre in Glasgow who he couldn't afford to pay."

"Well, it's definitely on my list."

Raymond took a sip from the glass and looked at his friend. "Something's up, isn't it?"

Simon laughed. "What do you mean?"

"Come on, Simon. It's no good. You can't pull the wool over my eyes. I can see that you're all tense. You're not yourself. You can tell me."

Simon took a long sip of the amber nectar and looked into his glass. "There's no hiding anything from you, is there, Raymond?" He took another sip. "Yes. Something's up, and I don't know what to do, Raymond."

Chapter 36

"Hello, Bernard, it's Adrian Drummond from Cadbury's."

"Hi there, Adrian. How are you?"

"All the better for seeing the fabulous script by Brian and Angus that Douglas presented to Dan and Caroline earlier. I have to say, Bernard, that we are terribly impressed by the speedy turn-around. I think it's the first time any agency has ever got back to us within two days of receiving a TV brief. And the other good bit of news is that we feel so confident with this one that we're not going to put it into research, and Harry is more than happy to save the company the additional expense. In fact, there's a big internal debate going on as we speak about the reliability of some of these research groups. But anyway, I just wanted to touch base and let you know from the horse's mouth as it were that everyone is very happy with this one and that from our point of view, Gordon Deedes Rutter is very much flavour of the month. So jolly well done, you. Now, I'm afraid I must dash off to a board meeting. Why don't I bell you later in the week to arrange lunch at the RAC Club?"

"Yes, that will be lovely ..." The line went dead. Bernard didn't even have a chance to say goodbye. Adrian was a very senior executive at Cadbury's and was something of a bulldozer. You could rarely get a word in edgeways. But on this occasion, there were no words to get in edgeways or any other way. Bernard was utterly bemused. What on earth had he been rabbiting on about? No work had been produced or presented to anyone. Or at least he hadn't seen anything. He tried calling Douglas but there was no answer. Then he called Magnus and Penny answered.

"Hello, you're through to the creative department. Can I help?"

"Hi, Penny. It's Bernard. Is Magnus around?"

"I'm afraid he's in a meeting with John and Shena. Can I leave a message?"

"How about Angus and Brian? Are they home or playing away this afternoon?"

"Their door is half closed and Angus has his feet up by the looks of things. So they'll be busy."

"Okay. I'll come down."

"I'm very well. Thanks for asking." It was no use — the line had already gone dead.

***

Bernard generally didn't let his annoyance show. He was usually seen as the calmest member of the team in a crisis. But on this occasion, the fact that he'd been left out of the loop entirely, really got his hackles up.

He stepped into Brian and Angus's office without knocking.

Angus looked up. "You've just interrupted my train of thought. You could have tapped on that large wooden thing. It's called a door."

Bernard ignored Angus's irritation. "Look. Would you mind explaining what the fuck is going on with the Spira script?"

"What Spira script?" replied Angus.

"We haven't even received that brief from your bus conductor yet. What are you talking about?" asked Brian.

"Yeah," added Angus. "We were a bit late for the briefing the other day, admittedly. So we thought, never mind, if we hang around a bit longer, three briefs will probably turn up at once. But not a bloody dicky-bird."

Bernard looked puzzled. "So you haven't written a script?"

"No," replied Angus. "And it doesn't look too likely that we're going to if you are going to barge in here willy-nilly interrupting the creative flow."

Bernard felt stupid. "Sorry, lads. I'm just confused."

"Look, just don't stand there. Take the weight off your feet." Angus looked at Brian. "Offer the man a drink, Brian. Looks like he needs one. What do we have in?"

"I can offer you a nice glass of Warres port," said Brian. "I don't think you'd appreciate the Cow & Gate condensed baby milk."

Bernard made a face. "God no. I didn't know you were working on that."

"No. Nor did we until half an hour ago," said Angus.

Bernard took a seat and Brian handed him a glass of Warres. "You look a bit stressed, Bernard. What's going on?"

Bernard took a sip and leaned back into the sofa. "Yes, I am, and frankly, I haven't got a clue ... I just received a call from Adrian Drummond, the senior client over at Cadbury's. The man was ecstatic. Happy as a dog with two dicks. Says they love Brian and Angus's script that was presented by Douglas earlier. And says it's all approved. Then he hung up. I didn't have a chance to ask any questions. But then, even if I had done, I don't think I could have asked anything without looking stupid."

"What!" exclaimed Angus in disbelief.

"So where is our bus conductor?" asked Brian.

Bernard shrugged. "I have no idea. He's out of the office."

Angus suddenly removed his feet from his desk. "Hang on one minute. What did we do with that joke script, Bry?"

"We didn't do anything with it. It was on your desk next to your telephone."

Angus started frantically shuffling through paperwork next to his telephone. "Here it is." He looked at Brian. "Fuck. You don't think ..."

"He might have ..."

"Would you care to explain in words of one syllable what's going on here?" said Bernard.

Angus looked at Bernard with trepidation. He was just about to say something but was interrupted by a tapping at the door.

Douglas's grinning face appeared at the doorway. "Hello, chaps. I have some good news."

Chapter 37

Reverend Granger stood at the pulpit.

"Beloved congregation of the Lord Jesus Christ.

"Today I'd like to reflect upon two powerful symbols of compassion and kindness that have resonated worldwide. One we know from the *New Testament* and the other we know from our television screens and newspapers. I refer, of course, to the parable of the Good Samaritan and the inspiring work of Bob Geldof and his creation of Band Aid. While these two might seem unrelated at first, they are in fact so very similar. Both demonstrate the transformative power of love and selflessness in an uncaring world. And they both serve as reminders that it is within our reach to bring hope and healing to those in need.

"In the *Gospel of Luke*, we encounter the timeless parable of the Good Samaritan. It tells the story of a man who fell victim to robbers, left half-dead on the side of the road, and ignored by those who passed by — until a stranger, a Samaritan, showed him mercy and compassion. This tale challenges us to examine our own hearts and asks: are we willing to extend our hand to those in desperate situations? Are we ready to step out of our comfort zones and become agents of healing?

"Today it has taken a group of musicians, led by Bob Geldof, to combat the devastating famine in Ethiopia. Their rallying cry, 'Do They Know It's Christmas?', has united people from all walks of life to address a humanitarian crisis. Not only has Band Aid succeeded in raising substantial funds, it has also captured the attention of the world, awakening our collective consciousness to the power of unity and compassion.

"Just as the Good Samaritan risked his reputation and resources to help a stranger in need, Bob Geldof and his colleagues have challenged the prevailing apathy of our times and become a beacon of hope. They have set a magnificent example by extending love and support to the stranger who is suffering, marginalised and in need.

"In a world filled with selfishness, envy and greed, may the legacy of the Good Samaritan and the spirit of Band Aid inspire us to embrace our shared humanity and be agents of hope, healing and transformation.

"And let us say, Amen."

Chapter 38

The club wasn't as large as Angus imagined it would be, but the atmosphere was exactly as a jazz club should be. There was a buzz to the place. The air was filled with banter, laughter and cigarette smoke. A hush descended as a grey-haired man in a black polo neck and denim jeans strode onto the stage and took hold of the microphone.

"You don't seem very impressed. Why don't you all hold hands and see if you can contact the living?"

This caused much hilarity and there was a round of enthusiastic clapping.

"That's a bit more like it. Anyway, in just a few moments whatshisname will be back on the stand. Meanwhile, our waiters and waitresses will be pleased to take you — er — to take care of you. We do, as a matter of fact, have six very good waiters and waitresses in the club. Between them, they have a job opening a bag of crisps, but they're great. There's one of our waiters moving ... that's Enrico, moving slowly but moving ... Enrico's Italian — doesn't speak any English. He came to this country three years ago and couldn't speak a word of English. Took a job in a Jewish restaurant ... Thought he was learning English ... Now he speaks great Yiddish and Italian ... but no English. He got married three weeks ago and already he can hear the patter of tiny feet ... his mother-in-law's a dwarf. He was telling me he had a row with his wife recently and she said 'What would you do if you came home and found a man in bed with me?' and Enrico said, 'I'd kick his guide dog.' Not bad for an Italian ... We also had a Hungarian waiter working here recently. He didn't understand the social security system and he used to stick Green Shield stamps on his national insurance card. He got nicked for it — the judge gave him six months, and a tea set."

Brian leaned over to Linda and whispered in her ear. "They are funny the first time, but he tells the same gags every time. But you can forgive him when he picks up the saxophone. He plays beautifully but doesn't perform very often. To be honest, I think it's a shame. I suppose he feels like he's in the shadow of such great players. They get all the big names playing here. Not bad for a little Jewish fella from the East End."

Linda laughed. "Brian Finkle, you don't have to tell me about Ronnie Scott. I know all about him. My dad used to cut his hair when he had a barber's shop in Soho. Dad was an amateur trumpet player and was very good friends with Ron."

"I had no idea. You kept that quiet."

"Yeah, well, some of us don't like to name-drop. And besides, I haven't seen much of dad since he and mum divorced. So he doesn't often pop up in my conversations. But dad used to be on friendly terms with both the famous and the infamous. He even knew the Kray twins."

"Blimey. You wouldn't want to give either of them a bad haircut."

Linda touched his nose fondly. "No, you wouldn't." She kissed him and then turned to Sam. "I hope you and Angus are enjoying this place. It's not everyone's cup of tea." Linda felt underdressed in Sam's company. She always wore the most stylish designer labels and looked so sophisticated, but she wasn't showy or pretentious.

"You must be joking, Linda. I love jazz." She'd actually been introduced to it by Marcus, her former boyfriend who'd been a brilliant jazz pianist. But Marcus had tragically died two summers ago from the sudden onset of a particularly aggressive form of lung cancer. The fact that he had never once smoked a cigarette made the wretched disease seem particularly cruel. She didn't like talking about Marcus in public. It was just too painful. She'd told Angus all about him, naturally, and had shared loads of photos and stuff. He and Marcus would almost certainly have got on like a house on fire. They both shared the same madcap sense of humour. It's probably why she was with Angus now. Besides, Marcus's last discernible words from his hospital bed had been, "Don't stay by yourself, Sam. Find someone else." If truth be known, Angus reminded her of Marcus, as did the jazz.

She wiped away a tear and forced a smile, and snuggled up to Angus. "I've been trying to convert muggins here to the cause. He probably won't admit it, but even he seems to be enjoying it. He hasn't stopped tapping his foot."

As Joe Pass and Oscar Peterson and their drummer and bass player returned to the stage, the place erupted in applause and cheers.

In the far corner, a young man in a smart grey suit with suede shoes poured a bottle of champagne into a young woman's glass and lit a cigar. He was a regular and would always stay to the end, which would usually be around 3.00 in the morning. As Minister of State for Health, his workload was mounting, but nothing would keep him away from this place. There were those in Parliament who visualised great things for this young jazz enthusiast. Some even thought he was Prime Ministerial material. He'd shrug off such suggestions in a typical self-effacing way that was so characteristic of the man.

Oscar Peterson switched on the microphone from his piano. "Well, thank you everyone for such an incredibly warm welcome. I can honestly say that of all the places I've played over the years, there's nothing in the world like playing here to you at Ronnie Scott's in London. This place feels like home to me. So thank you, Ronnie, for having us back again. Now, the next number we'd like to play has been dedicated to a man who has graced this place with his presence for some while now, despite his growing responsibilities. He knows who he is. He's sitting in his usual place in the far corner. Mr Kenneth Clarke. This one's for you. *My Little Suede Shoes* by the great Charlie Parker."

At another table, a group of City bankers shared a table with a man in a leather jacket who had just lit another cigarette and wasn't being especially sociable. The man had come here partly because he liked jazz but primarily because live music would usually calm his nerves. Sadly for him, he felt no calmer than when he stepped through the door. But then, Chaz had a lot to be anxious about.

Chapter 39

"Hello, Hugh. Look, thank you for the offer, but I can't accept it. I really can't."

"What do you mean, Simon? I don't need the money. You can't let this bastard blackmail you. I can write it off. You know I can. It's not a big deal ..."

"Well, it's a big deal for me. I won't be able to live with myself ..."

"For Christ's sake — sorry I didn't mean to say that. Just take the money, Simon. I can give you £5,000 straight up. Please. There are no strings attached ... I mean that. You can trust me, Simon."

"I know I can trust you. It's not about trust, Hugh. And I really do appreciate your offer of assistance. I'm really touched by it. It means more than you'll ever know. But I simply can't accept it."

"Well, look. I know you're a man of principle and all that. And I respect you for it. You know I do. But if you ever change your mind, the offer still stands. No strings."

"Thank you, Hugh. It means a lot. I have to go now." Reverend Granger put the phone down. He meant what he said, but the offer of £5,000 was tempting, he had to admit.

Chapter 40

"In all my years of running advertising agencies, this is the first time I've been asked to fire someone for winning business. In this case a substantial piece of business, with the prospect of winning more from the buggers." Kenneth Drayton sat at the head of the boardroom table and fiddled with his tie, which was always what he did when he was put on the spot.

Magnus wasn't going to let Kenneth say another word. "It's no good dressing this up as some incredible account win, Ken, and you know it. The guy is totally out of order. He has picked up a script and had the temerity of getting it retyped and presented to the client without me or anyone else in this fucking agency seeing it, let alone approving it. You can't operate an agency — any agency like that. It is outrageous and totally unacceptable. You know that."

Kenneth waited for Magnus to calm down.

"Do I have permission to speak?"

Magnus nodded.

"Yes, I do know that. Of course, he has behaved unacceptably. And yes, I will give him a bollocking. But we have something of a conundrum to deal with here, Magnus. Half an hour ago I had the head honcho of Cadbury's, Mike Latham, on the phone singing our praises and implying in the strongest terms that he'd like to see us handling a great deal more of their business. He even told me in confidence that they are furious with Saatchis and are looking to fire them. We are well placed to pick up some if not all of that business if we play our cards right. This could quite realistically become our largest piece of business. If we fire that tosspot Selby, and refuse to run the commercial on the grounds that it was created as some kind of cheap joke, we'll be jeopardising everything. Selby already has a relationship with the client from his time at Saatchis; it's the only reason I got him in here. And as far as I can gather, he and Dan Jiggins are like bloody brothers. They are both bus anoraks and apparently go to conventions together. I know this is not ideal but we've got to be realistic, Magnus.

"Apart from everything else, there's the worry I have about the Solid Fuel account. While our commercials are terrific and have given the agency a very high profile, there's no getting away from the fact that that bloody Thatcher woman is going to cock it all up for us. Look what she's doing to the coal industry, Magnus. I hate to say it, but we're living on borrowed time with that account. And Cadbury's couldn't have come along at a better time. We need that business, Magnus. As far as I'm concerned, it's a good, reliable, sustainable money-spinner."

Magnus wasn't happy but appreciated the dilemma that stared them in the face. As he weighed everything up in his head, there was a knock at the door. It was Penny.

"Sorry to interrupt. There are a couple of things here that need your signature pronto."

"That's fine," said Magnus. "Come in, Pen, and take a seat." She could tell that the atmosphere was tense. Kenneth was looking into space and twiddling his tie, which was always a bit of a giveaway. "Pen. Can I ask you for your honest opinion?" She nodded. "Well, we have a dilemma. The new boy Douglas has gone and sold a crap script that Angus wrote as a joke and the client thinks it's the best thing since sliced bread and wants us to make it. What would you do?"

"Ooh. I say. That's a bit tricky. You can't tell the client it was written as a joke because that'll make them look stupid. The good thing is that you have a happy client on your hands. I wouldn't want to change that. I think I'd live the lie and try and make the script better by executing it in an interesting way. Oh, and I'd definitely have a word with Douglas. He can't present work that hasn't been signed off. That's outrageous."

Kenneth smiled. "Well said, Penny."

Magnus nodded. "Yeah. Thanks, Pen. Painful though it is to admit, you're probably right. Do you think I should hand the poisoned chalice to Angus and Brian?"

"Well, if anyone was going to turn a terrible commercial into something decent, my money's on those two. And it is their script, after all," she added.

"To be fair, I don't think Brian had anything to do with it."

"How bad is it anyway?"

"It's an enormous steaming turd, Pen. And now I'm going to have to ask them to go away and polish it."

Chapter 41

"Hello. Reverend Granger speaking."

There was a pause and Granger could hear breathing on the other end of the line. It was him. He knew he'd call but it had still brought him out in a cold sweat. He closed the door.

"Do you have the money?"

"Yes."

"Good. Now listen carefully. You will place it in a holdall and leave it in a blue security locker at King's Cross station. Then you'll post the key and number to Chaz at The Dog and Duck, 18 Bateman Street, Soho, London W1D 3AJ. Once I have the money, the prints and negatives will be destroyed."

"No. That's not good enough. I won't risk putting all that money in a flimsy locker. And I want to see the photos destroyed with my own eyes. I don't trust you. If you don't comply, we don't have a deal. I'll go to the police and face the consequences. And if I lose my job as a result, so be it. I could always go back to lecturing. I still have all my contacts. In fact, I've been toying with the idea for some while."

"You're bluffing."

"There's only one way you'll ever find out. And that could be costly. Very costly."

There was a long pause. Granger might have pushed him too hard. Was he really prepared to go to the police? Almost certainly not. It would destroy his marriage. He was gay but he did love his wife. The last thing he'd be prepared to do was hurt her. She didn't deserve that.

"You're a demanding little shit, aren't you? ... Alright, I'll deliver the photos and negatives. And you can destroy them any fucking way you like. We need a discreet location at night."

"There's a discreet hotel at six Frith Street. It's called the Linton. I'll be in room four at 7.00 pm tomorrow. Do we have a deal?"

"We have a deal."

The line went dead.

Chapter 42

"I'm not convinced that Magnus is right about Melissa Bartlett, Bry."

Brian had his head in an overhead grant projector in the far corner of their office and was creating a poster layout for Cow & Gate. His disembodied voice echoed in the lightbox. "Doesn't sound like she needs the dough, though, does it?"

"I wouldn't be so sure. If Sam's anything to go by, women can never have enough filthy lucre at their disposal. You should see Sam's wardrobe. You must see that with Linda as well, surely."

"Yeah. I used to have two wardrobes to myself before I met Linda. Now all I have is half a wardrobe."

"Half a wardrobe? Count yourself lucky, mate. I have a sock drawer."

"But Melissa Bartlett already has all that stuff and will no doubt get given a load of gear by the fashion houses she models for. And she couldn't have strangled him, Angus."

"No, of course not. But she could have paid someone to do it for her. She had a lot to gain from doing so. Probably a few million quid."

"I guess that's a lot of wardrobes."

"Or a whole new fashion house with her name on the door."

Angus needed his first cigarette of the day and eagerly fumbled in his denim jacket that Brian nicknamed his DJ. As he did so, there was tapping on the door. "Okay. You can come in. We're decent. Nobody's having sex in here at the minute. Unless Brian's having it away inside the grant projector."

It was Magnus. "Morning, chaps. Sorry to barge in so early, but can we have a chat?"

Angus offered him a cigarette. "Thanks, but no thanks. I've given up again." He slumped into the sofa, which was annoyingly so much more comfortable than the one in his office. "I had a heated discussion last night with Ken. I went in there all guns blazing, which in hindsight probably wasn't the right thing to have done. Anyway, I roped Penny into the discussion to calm everyone's nerves and to hear what she thought."

"Good move, Maggers. Pen's a good egg."

"Not that I'd ever tell her to her face, but she's almost certainly the brightest person in this bloody place — present company excluded, of course. Anyway, the consensus is that we are going to have to produce the script in some form. And the reasons all relate, as you'd expect, to financial gain, which will be significant; not to mention the fact that we also have a very happy client on our hands who is now apparently threatening to give us more business."

"What's going to happen to that prize pillock, Selby?" asked Angus.

Magnus chuckled. "I was waiting for you to ask me that. I wanted Ken to fire him. But he says we can't. Selby's relationship with one of the senior clients is too close."

"What? Are they shagging or something?"

"It's worse than that, Angus. They go to bus, tram and railway conventions together."

"Christ."

"Now, the interesting thing that Penny said is that she thought there might be a way of producing this crap commercial in a really interesting and unusual way."

"It's a good suggestion, Magnus," said Brian.

"I'm glad you said that, Brian, because I thought so too," said Magnus.

"It's pretty much what Benson and Hedges did with their surreal campaign," added Brian. "I mean, there was no idea behind the work. The idea if you like was that there wasn't one. It was beautifully photographed and those images have become some of the best known and best loved in the business but there's no real thinking behind it."

"Some of us," added Angus, "call that style over substance."

"Didn't stop them winning shed loads of awards, though, did it?" argued Brian.

"And killing God knows how many poor sods with lung cancer. But I don't think we want to go there," said Angus as he took a long drag on his cigarette.

"So the question I have to ask you guys is this: do you fancy rising to the challenge?"

Angus looked at Brian. "You're the art director, Brian. It's your call."

Brian smiled. "Yeah. We'll do it. Leave it with us, Magnus."

"Thanks, boys. I knew I could count on you. Now, before I leave you in peace, I just wanted to update you on the Simple Soap front. Ian and Keith are coming in later. As you know, they are over the moon with the commercial and Keith now wants to take all three of us for lunch at Keith's club."

"Sounds posh," said Brian.

"It is. It's the Athenaeum in Pall Mall," said Magnus. "Now for the bad news. They don't let scruffy bastards like us in. So we're all going to have to nip out now and get ourselves jackets and ties."

Chapter 43

It was still light as he emerged from the tube station on Tottenham Court Road. Number six Frith Street was an elegant Georgian townhouse that was run as a smart hotel catering primarily to business executives. Room four was on the first floor. Chaz climbed the steep stairs that had been carpeted with a particularly deep pile that his feet sank into. He carried the prints and negatives in a large brown envelope.

The door to number four was ajar. He tapped on it lightly and entered. "Hello. Anyone at home?"

"I'm in the sitting room. Close the door behind you."

The voice sounded a little different to the voice he remembered hearing on the telephone. But telephones could be deceptive — they could do that. He switched the lights on but, irritatingly, they didn't work. He didn't like this. It didn't feel right. He reached inside his pocket and was comforted by the cold steel of his knife. He had never had to rely on it before, but it was always there for emergencies should the need arise.

Chapter 44

The Athenaeum was indeed posh and imposing. Its blue and white Grecian frieze that ran above its second storey had been copied from the Parthenon and was capped by an enormous golden statue of Minerva looking out over the Mall with her ever-watchful eye.

Brian looked up at its magnificence as all three of them mounted the steps. "No wonder we had to dress up. It makes a nice change from Jimmy the Greek's."

They were shown up a sweeping marble staircase to the grand dining room strangely known as the Coffee Room, and there by the window sat Keith and Ian who rose from their chairs.

"Dear boys. It's so lovely to see you."

"What a magnificent setting," said Magnus.

"Isn't it just? I've only recently become a member," replied Keith. "But it's not at all easy to join the place. Makes the MCC look like a doddle." A waiter approached the table and took their orders.

"Now, before we tuck into lunch, I just wanted to let you chaps know that our sales figures are going gangbusters and the commercial has only been aired for a week. In fact, most of our spots have been booked for next month. So huge thanks all round. It's a terrific piece of work."

Ian leaned forward. "And in terms of numbers, our sales in London alone have jumped this month already by an astonishing 65 per cent. We've never known anything remotely like this before. We haven't invested in any sales promotion, so we can only put it down to our television advertising campaign on Channel 4."

"I think that calls for a glass of bubbly, don't you, Ian?" added Keith.

Ian gesticulated to the waiter who immediately came to the table. "We'll have a bottle of your finest champagne, please."

Chapter 45

Svati had only taken the job to tide her over. She'd been the first in her family to go to university, but even with a grant, she needed some extra income to pay for sundries. Being a chambermaid wasn't exactly glamorous, but it was a pleasant environment in which to work and her employer paid reasonably well. She'd learnt the value of hard work from her parents, who had come to this country in the late 50s and built their small business from scratch.

She had unlocked the store cupboard and removed the bowl of cleaning products and the vacuum cleaner. Now she'd collect the keys for the first floor from reception. But at reception, she couldn't understand why she could only find the keys to rooms one, two and three. The key to room four was nowhere to be seen. So there was no way round it, she'd have to use the emergency universal key.

She inserted this universal key into the look. Thankfully, it turned and the lock made a satisfactory clunk. Strangely, the room was very dark, so she switched on the lights but the gloom persisted. How annoying. She'd have to go back to the store cupboard to retrieve some light bulbs. It could wait. She'd draw the curtains in the entrance lobby first and then change the bedsheets. As daylight from the side window flooded the lobby, she was mystified that the two table lamps were lacking light bulbs. How peculiar that any guest would want to steal light bulbs. There were some very strange people around. She opened the bedroom door and yet again the curtains had been drawn closed and the light switch was failing to work. She strode over to the window and pulled open the curtains, and that's when she spotted him.

She froze. But couldn't take her eyes off him. She'd never seen a dead person before. He was sitting upright in the armchair, fair unkempt hair, unshaven jowls, eyes wide open and mouth gaping. In the centre of his forehead was a perfect small circle of dark red, congealed blood. He didn't look like a typical guest. He wasn't wearing a suit and tie for a start. Instead, he wore a t-shirt, jeans and a black leather jacket that had seen better days. On the floor in front of him was a large brown envelope. She stooped and picked it up. It was empty.

She left everything in place and made her way to the manager's office in the basement.

"Hello, luv. Are you alright? You look very pale. Are you feeling alright?"

She slumped into a chair. "It's room four ... There's a dead man in room four."

***

Chief Inspector Goldman knelt in front of the dead body. He wasn't a ballistics expert, but it looked to him as if the bullet would have entered the man's forehead from a low angle. And there was another chair in the room opposite him. His hunch was that the man had been shot by someone sitting in the other chair. The gun could have been concealed. The other obvious observation concerned the drawn blinds and curtains and the fact that all the light bulbs had been removed and placed in a wastepaper basket. So it looked as if the murderer had shot his victim in very low light conditions with one very precise bullet to the forehead. This looked like a very professional job by a marksman.

He'd wait here while officers taped off the area. The forensic team would arrive any minute now to scour the scene and take photos. He'd always sound them out about his own theories and five times out of ten he'd be spot on the money. He was feeling fairly confident that he was about to get it right today.

Chapter 46

Reverend Granger dumped the old copies of *The Times* on the bonfire next to his vegetable plot. The orange flames were beginning to lick the newsprint and turn it brown. As the heat began to build, he removed a copy of *The Christian Chronicle* from beneath his jumper and discreetly pulled out the photos. They were repulsive and made him feel dirty. Whoever photographed them deserved to rot in hell. Nobody had the right to invade his privacy like that and attempt to ruin his life. He placed them back inside the newspaper and threw them onto the bonfire as it crackled and glowed and threw up the odd piece of charred black newsprint into the morning breeze. He felt the tenseness in his entire posture ease up. He could relax now. Everything was under control.

He stepped back inside the house and went upstairs to the loft. He hadn't picked up a cricket bat for some considerable while but the idea of playing a match at the Hurlingham Club certainly appealed to him. He needed a distraction. He hadn't managed to sleep for several nights now. The whole sordid blackmailing thing had shaken him to his core. He couldn't just let that piece of vermin shatter everything he'd managed to build up over the years. He'd never outwardly compare human beings to disease-ridden rodents. But in truth, it was the only way to describe people like that. You had to treat them like vermin, too.

"Darling, are you alright up there?" It was his wife calling from the kitchen downstairs.

He poked his head through the hatch opening to the loft. "I'm fine. I'm just in the loft looking for my cricket bag." That seemed to satisfy her as he heard her pick up the phone and begin to chat away. It would probably be her sister.

The large leather bag was lodged beneath a suitcase and had collected dust. He unzipped it and pulled out a pair of leather pads that still displayed grass stains from his university days. He buried his nose in the soft buckskin and could almost smell the freshly cut grass of the outfield and in his mind's eye could picture the scene and hear that distinctive sound of leather on willow.

***

He'd heard good things about the Hurlingham Club ground but had never had the pleasure of playing on it until today. The setting certainly met with his approval. The place clearly had history and the ground was undeniably pretty.

Reverend Simon Granger had arrived early and parked himself on one of the many cane chairs that had been placed out on the terrace where he now nursed a coffee. There were a couple of elderly cardigan-wearing members reading the newspaper in this haven of tranquillity. Granger closed his eyes momentarily, and was brought to his senses by a familiar-sounding voice.

"I'm assuming it's Reverend Granger."

Granger opened his eyes.

"Sorry, I didn't mean to disturb you. I'm Roy. Roy Pickering. Very nice to put a face to a name." Roy shook him warmly by the hand and sat at the table. "I hope you didn't mind me asking you to do the honours today. Robin was quite insistent that I asked you. He would dearly love to have been here with us."

Granger shook his head. "No. Not in the least. In fact, I was saying to Gillian my wife earlier that a game of cricket would do me the world of good. I haven't picked up a cricket bat since university days."

A smart-looking waiter arrived and deposited a coffee and a plate of croissants and strawberry jam. Roy gestured towards the plate. "Do tuck in. This place is my second home I'm afraid. The food here is terribly good. Even the jam is homemade. Robin says you are a bit of an all-rounder."

Granger laughed. "I used to be. But I'm bound to be a bit rusty."

Roy tore open a croissant. "I've heard that one before. How do you feel about opening the innings?"

Granger shrugged. "I used to open the innings, but that was an awfully long time ago."

"You'll be fine. The opposition is only a motley bunch of advertising and entertainment bods. Two of our lads are in the advertising game and they've cobbled a team together. With the best will in the world, I don't think we'd be able to class them as anything other than weak at best. I understand that one of their chaps is American and doesn't even know what cricket is."

"Well, in that case, I will happily accept the challenge. Now, to change the subject, as far as the memorial service is concerned, I thought I'd just say a few words by way of a tribute to Benjamin Bartlett and include Psalm 23 before scattering the ashes."

"That sounds perfect. Ben's wife Melissa will say a few words and I will do likewise. But after your piece, we'd like to kick off with a piece of music by Clifford, who plays the double bass for the London Symphony Orchestra."

"I don't suppose there can be many pieces written for solo double bass."

"No, I shouldn't think there are, but Clifford is also pretty nifty on the ivories. He'll be playing something on the piano. Then following everyone's contributions, there'll be a light lunch and the match will start at around 1 o'clock."

Granger nodded and finished his coffee.

***

Angus, Brian and Magnus took their seats at the back of the Terrace Room. It was a lovely space with the feel of a conservatory due to a glazed frontage and partially glazed roof extension, which afforded its occupants a very agreeable view of the manicured grounds. As they settled in their seats, a tall man in glasses and a dog collar took his place behind a lectern.

"First of all, welcome to this lovely setting. Today we gather to pay tribute to Benjamin Bartlett. It's an incredibly sad and poignant day. Ben, as you know, loved this place and that's why Ben's wife Melissa thought it fitting to spread her husband's ashes here — the place where Ben was in his element. For him the Hurlingham Club cricket ground was hallowed turf. It was heaven on earth. So I am going to ask all of you to follow Melissa and myself onto the cricket ground where we will conduct a short ceremony and Melissa will release Ben's ashes where Ben would always open the batting."

Melissa appeared at Reverend Granger's side carrying a small urn and as they stepped out into the sunshine, everyone followed in silence.

The party followed in a procession across the lawns and then formed a circle around the wicket.

Roy was feeling a little anxious. He hadn't actually spoken to the club about their little ceremony and it now occurred to him that the management may not have approved. Fortunately, there were enough of them to shield proceedings from prying eyes.

Reverend Granger stood beside the stumps. "As we mourn the loss of Benjamin Bartlett, let us all celebrate the indelible mark he left on all who knew and loved him. Several people here are going to share with us their memories of their dear friend shortly, but first of all, I'm going to recite a few words followed by Psalm 23. And then Melissa will release her husband's ashes.

"As we bid farewell to Benjamin Bartlett, let us cherish the memories and life lessons he has gifted us. May his soul find eternal rest, and may we honour his memory by continuing to uphold the values he exemplified on and off the pitch.

"In this time of loss, we offer our heartfelt condolences to Benjamin's family and friends. May we find strength in each other's support and the comforting words of the Psalms as we navigate through this difficult time.

"I'd now like to ask Melissa to release Ben's ashes."

Melissa stepped forward, tears streaming down her cheeks causing her eye mascara to run. She removed the lid and held the urn upside down and a pale grey cloud wafted across the cricket pitch and dispersed.

Reverend Granger removed his glasses and closed his eyes.

"The Lord is my shepherd; I shall not want.

He makes me lie down in green pastures.

He leads me beside quiet waters.

He restores my soul.

He leads me in paths of righteousness for his name's sake ..."

***

By the time they had returned, the room had been transformed. A sea of round tables dressed with white linen tablecloths were laden with plates of quiche, cold meats, salmon and umpteen varieties of exotic looking salads.

Reverend Granger encouraged everyone to take a seat. He placed his glasses on his nose and referred to his notes. "Ladies and gentlemen. Please do take a seat wherever you like. Before enjoying lunch, which has been very generously provided by Melissa Bartlett, Clifford would like to share a piece of music that would have resonated with Ben. And following Clifford's performance, Melissa and Roy are going to say a few words. So, now I'm going to shut up and hand you over to Clifford."

Clifford, who was already seated at the grand piano, stood and faced his audience. "Thank you, Reverend, for stepping in at the last minute and conducting such a moving ceremony. I think Ben would have loved every moment of it. Now, some of you may have known that Ben was a bit of a jazz buff on the quiet, and like me, was a great admirer of the American composer and pianist Bill Evans. So I thought it would be fitting to play a piece titled *We Will Meet Again* that Bill Evans wrote in 1979 following the suicide of his brother Harry. He dedicated this piece to Harry and it was, in fact, the last studio recording that Bill Evans ever made. Sadly, Evans himself died the following year. He was only 51 years of age — the very same age as our dear departed friend. And the album in which this piece appears won Bill Evans a Grammy award posthumously the following year. I know that Ben loved this album because he had it in his studio and according to Melissa, he often played it when he was taking photographs. So dear Ben, wherever you are, this one's for you." Clifford turned to the piano, adjusted the height of the piano stool, composed himself and gently wiggled his fingers above the keys of the Steinway. He paused for a few moments. He was an excellent pianist and was used to playing in public to far larger numbers, but for some curious reason, he felt incredibly nervous. He took a deep breath and then began to play.

Brian had heard some of Bill Evans' work but wasn't at all familiar with this piece, which Clifford played beautifully with such feeling that it moved him beyond words. And as the very last note resonated and hung in the air, the entire audience sat in complete silence, stunned by the mellifluous chords, rhythms and poetry of Clifford's rendition. The silence was eventually and slowly punctured by a standing ovation that grew in intensity. Clifford rose from his seat, bowed and returned to his place at the table, and Reverend Granger took his place by the piano.

"Thank you, Clifford. That was simply beautiful and incredibly moving. And now I'd like to ask Melissa to share with us her memories of her husband."

Melissa tentatively stepped forward and Granger lightly held her upper arm as a supportive and caring gesture. She smiled and looked out into the sea of faces without really focussing on any of them.

"First of all, I'd like to thank each and every one of you for coming here today. It means a lot. Far more than any of you could possibly know. And Clifford, that performance was so sublime, it made me cry. So thank you. Ben would have loved it.

"I actually wrote a speech, but I'm not going to use it. I'm just going to speak from the heart.

"Ben could be a difficult, irritating and thoughtless bastard at times."

There were a couple of nervous laughs. "As you know, our marriage was in the process of falling apart. But the funny thing was that despite everything, we still quite liked each other. You see, Ben was basically a good bloke. He was funny, kind, and he was talented — bloody talented. And even though we'd become tired of each other, I still cared for him, and we still looked out for each other. And I still enjoyed hearing that voice of his leaving cheeky messages on my answer phone. Of course, when we first met and got married back in 1978, I loved him to bits. There can't be many people on this planet who have been proposed to in an elevator that had become stuck between two floors at Harrods, but that's how he proposed to me. I discovered later that he'd contrived to have the lift stop between floors by persuading the store owner to go along with this ruse. But that was Ben all over. And if I'm honest, I don't expect there'll be anyone else I'll ever love as much as I used to love that man. And I know how much he meant to you lot. He was loyal to his friends and supportive of those who needed support. He'd often give money to homeless people in the gutter. On one occasion I remember him taking a street busker to lunch at the Savoy because he thought the guy was talented and deserved a break. And he was never arrogant. Self-effacing, yes. Lacking in confidence, absolutely. But arrogant, never.

"Though we'd have been divorced, we would have still remained good friends and he'd still have been an important part of my life. Of that I have no doubt at all. Ben didn't deserve to meet his end in the terrible way he did. Nobody deserves that. And I can't imagine who would want to do that to him. And that will no doubt haunt me for the rest of my years.

"So Ben, if you're listening, I hope you are at peace. Your memory will live on.

"God bless."

As Melissa returned to her seat, there was much dabbing of moist eyes and quiet sobs. Roy slowly rose from his seat and sat on the piano stool and waited a few moments for everyone to regain their composure. He spoke softly and compassionately in the same way he might have addressed a young teenager from a broken home who now faced a conviction for murder.

"In all my years as a criminal barrister faced with dealing with the terrible aftermath of trauma of the worst kind, this is by far the most difficult trauma for me to deal with, because, of course, I can't be detached from it.

"Dear Ben was a really close friend. We'd known each other for many years. In many ways, we were so incredibly different. While I come from a horribly privileged background, he had an impoverished upbringing in Margate where he was taken into care by a teenage single mother who was deemed incapable and too poor to look after him. It was a cruel act by the authorities that took many years to rectify. When he was eventually reunited with his mother, she was the one who saw his potential and spurred him on. And I'm convinced that it was largely down to her that he went on to carve an incredible career for himself as a leading professional photographer. His early black and white portraits, many of which now hang on permanent display at the National Portrait Gallery, are powerful and full of humanity. If you haven't already seen them, I'd urge you to do so. His prodigious talent for image making and his meticulous and obsessive fascination for and with lighting will I'm sure be what his peers will remember him for. I've heard him referred to on several occasions as 'Vermeer with a camera'. And anyone who knows the works of Vermeer will be familiar with the ethereal quality of the light that the Dutch master manages to capture in his compositions. And it is the same quality of brilliant fleeting light that Ben's own images all bask in. It came to define his work and was what made him such a popular choice of photographer for some of the world's leading brands and their advertising agencies. He could talk for hours about his love of old 1930s Hollywood arc lights that were being jettisoned for harsh modern lights that were in his eyes no match for the former. And I have fond memories of helping him rescue these old lights from building skips when studios went bankrupt.

"Work aside, he was fantastic company: well read, funny, a great storyteller, and of course, a natural and elegant batsman. Cricket was a game he adored. And it pains me that we will never see any more of those inimitable cover drives of his. Then there was his sense of mischief that Melissa has already alluded to. I could regale you with countless stories about his antics, but one that always sticks in my memory and never fails to make me smile was the time he came into chambers to meet me for lunch and somehow managed to persuade the junior clerk that he suffered from Tourette's syndrome and was Mr Pickering's client who was defending him on charges of repeatedly disturbing the peace in the British Library Reading Room by repeatedly using the F word very loudly.

"Finally, I'd just like to mention his struggle with depression and the occasional manic episode. He was unusual in that he would openly talk about these issues, which so many people these days brush under the carpet, and in this sense I think he was incredibly brave, and although I never told him as much to his face, which I now regret, I admired him enormously for that.

"May God bless you, Benjamin Bartlett, and may you rest in eternal peace."

***

Reverend Granger passed the plate of cold meats to Magnus. "I understand that you are one of the advertising executives."

Magnus smiled. "Executive is a bit of a grand word. But, yes, the name's Magnus. Did you know Ben?"

"No. I'm afraid I didn't. In fact, I feel a bit of a fraud. I think I'm the only person here who didn't. And I have to confess that I haven't even seen his photographs."

Magnus giggled.

Granger looked a little nonplussed. "Sorry. Did I say something?"

"It's just the idea of a vicar making a confession. It amused me. Sorry."

"Oh, of course. That is quite funny."

"As for Ben's photographs, they are well worth seeing. They're not the kind of photographs you'd forget in a hurry. Like Roy says, you should check him out at the National Portrait Gallery. They are wonderful portraits. Quite haunting actually. Now, I hear you are opening the innings."

"I think that's the idea, but I haven't held a cricket bat since university days."

"Well, that's better than me. I've never held one full stop."

Chapter 47

"So have I managed to win you over, Shaggers?"

Angus was flicking through *The Guardian*. "Come again, squire."

"Have I turned you into a jazz nut?"

"Don't know about jazz nut, but yeah, I really enjoyed it. It's a great club with a fantastic atmosphere. And we'd certainly be up for a return visit."

Brian grinned. "Great. Good to know that I've won you over. By the way, there's a lovely little hotel at number six Frith Street. Linda and I thought we'd stay there next time. Saves trying to get a cab in the early hours."

"Sounds like a good idea. With hindsight, I think we were pretty lucky to get that cab ..." Angus suddenly went quiet as a piece in the newspaper caught his eye. "Bloody hell!"

"What's up?"

Angus folded the newspaper into quarters and handed it to Brian. "Looks like your hotel is in the news."

Brian eagerly took the newspaper thinking that it was some kind of review. Below a picture of the hotel a headline read: *Mystery murder in Soho.* He continued reading.

The Metropolitan Police are investigating the murder of a small-time crook in the heart of Soho. The body of Charles Adams, a fraudster who had served time in prison for posing as an antique dealer and defrauding elderly customers, was discovered in the early hours by a chambermaid working at the Linton Hotel at six Frith Street in the heart of Soho.

Detective Inspector Goldman, who is leading the investigation, has told The Guardian *that the victim had been shot in what looked like a gangland killing. "It's quite possible that he became embroiled in serious crime and was out of his depth. The killing was clearly the work of a professional hitman."*

The police investigation is ongoing.

Brian tossed the newspaper onto the table. "Christ, Shaggers. That's a bit bloody spooky. Another blinking murder so close to home. Do you think we're jinxed?"

***

Inspector Goldman sat in the basement office of the Linton Hotel. The man sitting before him had been the hotel manager for his entire working career. He was balding and in his late fifties with a distinctive Essex accent. He stirred his tea and took a sip. "As I say, Inspector, we had a booking for room four, which had been made over the phone. I took the call and I remember it because it was clearly made from a call box. I could hear the beeps and the money dropping in."

Inspector Goldman nodded. "And you say that the payment was received in the post two days later."

"That's correct. And it was in cash, which was unusual. I mean, who sends money in the post?"

"And the man who you spoke to on the phone, can you describe his voice?"

"I'd say he was my kind of age. Late 40s to early 50s. And I reckon he was a Londoner. Said his name was Brian Knox."

"But nobody checked in."

"That's right. And we never received a call to cancel the room either. The chambermaid was the one who realised that the key had gone missing. Still hasn't shown up. So whoever got into that room and shot that poor sod must have somehow got hold of the key."

"And you have a full list of guests staying on that fateful day?"

"Yes. I've typed up the list here." He handed Inspector Goldman a short list. There were only four names and addresses. "As you can see, it's pretty quiet at the moment."

"And you saw nobody other than these guests?"

"That's right. Our reception desk is behind the staircase, so someone could have come through the front door without being spotted and gone up to the first floor if they already had the key. Neither I nor our receptionist saw anyone other than those four people staying here."

"Thank you for your time, Mr Underhay." Inspector Goldman produced a card and handed it to the hotel manager. "If anything else comes to mind that you think might be helpful, just give me a call. No matter how small."

The other man smiled and took the card. "No problem, Inspector. It's a bit ironic, but we're getting a fancy video security camera installed at the front entrance on Thursday."

"Oh, well. Sod's Law, isn't it?"

***

As Inspector Goldman got back to his desk and removed his jacket, his phone began to ring.

"Hello. Inspector Goldman speaking."

"Hello, Inspector, it's Ian here. I have completed the forensic report. Essentially, your theory is correct. He was certainly shot from a low angle, and almost certainly from a seated position from the chair opposite — from a distance of around 15 feet. So the murderer could well be a marksman. The land and groove impressions on the removed bullet also tell us very clearly that the murder weapon was a Beretta 92 semi-automatic pistol fitted with a silencer.

"Everything points to a professional hit. There are no fingerprints. No microscopic traces on the body that could relate to the murderer, which suggests that he or she kept their distance intentionally. The full report is winging its way as we speak."

"That's great work, Ian. Thanks for letting me know."

Chapter 48

Brian was flipping through the Creative Handbook and making notes. "Bearing in mind that we have a happy client and quite a lot of money to spend on this crap script, I reckon we should produce something that looks stunning if nothing else."

"Sounds good to me, Finklebrain. So what are you thinking?"

"I've just seen some really interesting short animated films made by two guys in Bristol for Channel Four. They've gone and recorded some ordinary mundane conversations and then beautifully animated plasticine models to these real voices. It works really well. So our two characters sitting in the cinema commenting about the commercial on the big screen could be animated in the same way. And when we show the chocolate bar on the cinema screen, we could get it animated by a traditional two-dimensional animator. And I'm thinking of someone like Jimmy Murakami."

"Who he?"

"He, Shaggers, is the bloke who animated the Raymond Briggs' *Snowman* short film."

"Oh, wow. That was stunning."

"Exactly."

"Now, take a look at this."

Brian shoved a U-matic tape into the video machine and switched it on. The first short film was of a door-to-door salesman trying to sell his wares to an elderly couple — all animated in plasticine to a real conversation. And the second short film was of a disc jockey. Both films were full of comic little touches and were incredibly detailed.

"I love these, Brian," said Angus. "That opening scene with the disc jockey's bed folding out of the wall inside a sound studio with him in it is brilliant."

"Yeah, it's incredible, isn't it? Must have taken ages to animate."

"So who are these dudes?"

"Peter Lord and David Sproxton from some small company called Aardman Animation."

Chapter 49

"Beloved congregation of the Lord Jesus Christ.

"Today, I stand before you to share a message that touches the very essence of our existence — the sanctity of life. Life is a divine gift bestowed upon us, and it is our responsibility to cherish and respect it in all its forms. As we contemplate this profound truth, let us reflect on the significance and meaning of every life, from the moment of conception to the final breath.

"In the *Book of Genesis*, we read that God created humankind in His image. This divine image grants each one of us inherent value and purpose, regardless of our background, race or status. We are all uniquely individual, and it is this uniqueness that underscores the sanctity of life."

Reverend Granger paused and took a sip of water. The congregation was a particularly large one this Sunday, and most of them seemed to be awake. As the morning sun illuminated the stained-glass figures of Saint Francis and his ilk and threw puddles of blue and purple light onto the stone floor, he replaced the glass of water and continued.

"Life is a miracle, a wondrous tapestry woven by the hands of the Creator. Consider the complexity of the human body, the intricacy of every cell, and the harmony of each organ working together. From the tiniest organisms to the most intelligent beings, life is a symphony of existence that should inspire awe and reverence.

"As custodians of life, we are called upon to nurture and protect it. Whether it be our own lives, the lives of those we love, or the lives of strangers, we are entrusted with a sacred duty to promote well-being, offer compassion, and foster a culture of love and kindness.

"Each life is a journey of growth and transformation. We are all travellers on this road, facing different challenges, joys and sorrows. Let us remember that we are not alone and that every life is intertwined with others. Our actions towards others have ripple effects that can uplift or devastate. Therefore, we must choose the path of empathy and understanding.

"Life unfolds in seasons — birth, youth, adulthood and old age. Each phase has its unique beauty and significance. As we respect the sanctity of life, let us also honour the dignity and wisdom that comes with age, offering our care and support to those in their twilight years.

"Life is not without its trials and tribulations. Mistakes and regrets can burden our souls. However, the sanctity of life also encompasses the hope of redemption and the power of forgiveness. Let us extend grace to ourselves and others, recognising that every life is capable of change and growth.

"Beyond human life, let us not forget the sanctity of all living beings that share this planet with us. From the tiniest insects to the grandest animals, each life has a purpose in the intricate web of creation. As stewards of this world, we must protect and preserve these precious creatures.

"In conclusion, the sanctity of life is a profound truth that should resonate deeply within our hearts. We are called upon to treat every life with love, respect and dignity, as we recognise the divine spark that resides within each soul. Let us strive to create a world in which the sanctity of life is upheld, and where compassion and understanding guide our every action.

"May we live our lives as a testament to the preciousness of this gift, honouring the sacredness of life in all that we do.

"And let us say, Amen."

***

His wife stood beside him as he bid each and every one of them goodbye. Raymond Blunt and his wife in her wheelchair were the last of his congregants he shook warmly by the hand. "It's good of you both to come, Raymond. And I'm particularly honoured to see Susan here, too."

She smiled at him and nodded.

"We're off in a couple of days, Simon, for a couple of weeks in sunnier climes. I'll be in touch when we're back."

"How very sensible." Granger pulled a small volume from his cassock. "Here's a little something you'll enjoy while you're away."

Raymond took the book. It was entitled simply *William Byrd — a Biography*. "Thank you, Simon. How very thoughtful. I think it's only just come out."

Granger smiled. "Yes. I thought you'd appreciate it. You'll find Chapter Five particularly rewarding."

Reverend Granger and his wife watched their friends depart. "He's remarkable for his age, isn't he?"

He turned to his wife and kissed her. "Yes, he's much fitter than most men of his vintage. Strong as an ox, I think his army years served him well. Do you know, he goes to the gym every morning and still does 100 press-ups every day?"

"No ... I had no idea."

***

Raymond applied the brakes to his wife's wheelchair and then carried her with ease and gently deposited her onto the passenger seat of their Austin Maestro. Then he removed the cushion and footplates, folded the wheelchair, and placed everything on the back seat. This done, he closed the passenger door and returned to the driver's seat and closed his door. He held the small volume on his knees. Simon had placed a rubber band around it, which Raymond now removed. He turned to Chapter Five and removed the wad of fifty-pound notes. It was surprising how small £5,000 looked in fifties.

Chapter 50

They had placed adverts in *The Lady* with the intention of finding a couple of elderly people to read the mundane lines of Angus's script. And Brian had briefed Sid the casting director very thoroughly. They didn't want actors or anyone who sounded like they were acting. Authenticity was the name of the game, which is all very well in theory, but when it comes to actually finding voices that you think sound authentic without sounding dreadful, the task becomes rather difficult.

Angus and Brian had sat in the studio listening to countless readings, and none of them sounded quite right.

Brian made himself another black coffee as they waited for another couple to arrive. "Christ. I never thought it would be this difficult to cast for normal voices to read your banal script."

Angus looked a bit hurt. "Thanks a bunch … But it's alright. It always was banal, I know. You don't have to rub it in though."

"As the bishop said to the actress," added Brian.

"Sounds like you're turning into that camp comedian that Magnus had a curry with."

"Sorry. It wasn't intentional. How many more have we got to see, Sid?"

Sid looked up from his Filofax. "We only have one couple left." As he spoke these words, an elderly man and a woman in a wheelchair appeared at the doorway.

"Are you Raymond and Susan Blunt by any chance?" enquired Sid.

"Indeed we are," replied Raymond. "I do hope we're not too late."

Brian immediately liked the man's voice. It was naturally rich and resonant and had character. "No, that's fine. I think you're the last people we're hearing today."

The man smiled and then approached Brian and whispered in his ear. "My wife Susan has Parkinson's disease, so she doesn't really make conversation and her memory is shot to pieces, but she can read beautifully when she's given a script. I hope that's alright with you."

Brian was very touched that he had wanted his wife to have an opportunity. He clearly adored her and he seemed like such a lovely man. Brian had already decided there and then that he wasn't going to listen to anyone else. These two were going to fit the bill perfectly. He knew it instinctively and gave a discrete thumb-up to Angus.

Sid handed Raymond and Susan the script and led them into the recording booth behind glass. They both placed the earphones on and Sid spoke to them through the intercom system. "Okay, Raymond and Susan, you can begin to read whenever you're ready. We have the tape rolling now." Raymond began to read first, and his wife interjected perfectly. They sounded just like two lovely characters, which, of course, they were.

"Have you got that on tape, Sid?" asked Brian.

"Yeah."

"Brilliant. Can we hear it back please?"

Sid pressed the rewind and playback buttons and the voices came through the speaker system. Brian nodded approvingly. "What do you reckon, Angus?"

Angus laughed. "They're great. They actually make you smile. It's insane because on paper it's pathetic."

Brian turned to Sid. "We'll go with these two, Sid. Thanks." Then he went through to the recording booth to talk to Raymond and Susan. "Thank you very much for that. We'd like to use you for our commercial. We'd just like to do a couple of extra readings to be on the safe side. And then there is a bit of paperwork for you to sign. Is that alright?"

"That's terrific." And with that, Raymond looked at his wife. "Isn't that wonderful, Susan? They want to use us for their TV commercial." He laughed. "We're going to be famous."

Susan smiled. Then Raymond turned to Brian. "I don't wish to sound ungrateful, but I am supposing we will get paid for our efforts."

Brian felt bad. Nobody had explained anything to these two lovely people. "I'm sorry. Someone should have explained that you will receive a fee for today and an additional usage fee when the commercial goes out. Sid will give you all the details. But don't worry, you'll be very well paid."

Sid adjusted the sound levels on his console and then pressed the button to speak to the recording booth. "Okay, you lovely people. If you could pop your headphones back on, we'll do a couple more just like that, please." As Raymond and Susan read their lines for the last couple of times, a young receptionist popped her head around the door.

"Sorry to interrupt but I have a Penny on the phone to speak to Angus."

"No problem, I'll take it." Angus pulled himself from the leather sofa and let himself through the incredibly heavy door into the reception area and picked up the phone.

"Hi, Pen. Is everything okay?"

"Everything's fine. Just wanted to know what time you were heading back as we've got a cake for Brian's birthday and Magnus wants to do a bit of a presentation."

"Shouldn't be long here. We're just wrapping up now. It took all day to find the right voices, but the last two were perfect. They are just like your grandparents. Real sweeties."

Epilogue

As Brian got into the cab, he removed a copy of the *Evening Standard* that was lying on the seat. He couldn't help noticing the headline and he placed the folded newspaper on Angus's knees. "So much for your theory about Melissa Bartlett." The headline read: *Murder victim's wife donates £5 million to Cancer Research.*

Angus scanned the article: *The* Evening Standard *has learnt that Melissa Bartlett, the fashion model and wife of photographer Benjamin Bartlett who was brutally murdered last month, has made a donation of £5 million to the charity Cancer Research. "This is one of the largest private donations we have received," said Michael Hoxton, the charity's Managing Director. "And we are hugely grateful for Mrs Bartlett's incredible generosity. It will assist us greatly in our efforts to find a cure for this devastating disease." Further details inside.*

Angus threw the newspaper back onto the seat next to Brian and grunted. It was his way of admitting defeat. "Oh, I forgot to mention, Brian, that there's a little something for your birthday from the agency in the boardroom, so don't go without picking it up."

"Wow. I wasn't expecting that."

"Yeah. Magnus called earlier and told me. Didn't want you to go home without collecting it."

"Blimey. I wonder what they've got me?"

Angus shrugged. "Search me. New set of Magic Markers maybe."

The cab pulled up and they jumped out. "I'll go straight up to the boardroom then and pick up my Magic Markers. I'll be back down in a mo."

Angus smiled. "Sure. I'll see you in a bit."

Brian flew up the stairs two at a time and on the fourth floor pushed through the double doors and along the corridor to the boardroom. The place seemed unusually quiet. It was only 6 o'clock. There'd usually be a fair number of people still at their desks. He didn't think much about it as he pushed open the boardroom door and switched on the lights. As he did so he was greeted by 150 people all wearing party hats and whooping and screaming. Angus tapped him on his shoulder from behind. "Sorry, mate. I was sworn to secrecy. Happy birthday."

And then before he could catch his breath, Linda appeared from nowhere and kissed him on the lips as a rendition of Elton John's *Rocket Man* reverberated through the speakers.

"Fancy meeting you here. Do you come here often?"

Brian laughed. He couldn't believe he'd fallen for it, but was so incredibly happy that he had. He loved this place.

Magnus kicked off his shoes and climbed onto the boardroom table and then began to tap on a champagne flute with a spoon. The hubbub began to subside and the music was turned down.

"Ladies and gents, as you all know, today is Brian's birthday. Brian has been with us for just over a year and in this very short period has, with his partner in crime, made a massive contribution to this agency. So this surprise party is our way of just saying thank you. It's been a fantastic year and a bit, and on a personal level, I look forward to working with you for many years to come. And in order to cement some kind of loyalty to this place, and stop that bastard Tom Haggard down the road from poaching you, we have contrived to rustle up some coffers and buy you a birthday present. Can I call on my able assistant to do the presentation?"

Penny appeared from the back of the room with a flat package tied up with a red ribbon. She planted a kiss on Brian's cheek and presented him with his present. "Here you go, Birthday Boy."

Brian took hold of the package and began to open it. It was a rather lovely framed picture.

"Brian, if you didn't know," continued Magnus, "has a thing about Victorian artists. So while pottering down the road the other day I came across an interesting little place off the Charing Cross Road selling antiques. The owner assures me that this is a limited edition print by the Victorian watercolourist Myles Birket Foster. I thought the quality was particularly good. And the framing and mounting are, I think, very impressive. Anyway, I do hope you like it, Brian."

While Brian was listening, he had removed his glasses and was inspecting the picture up close. He couldn't quite believe what he was looking at. There was a spontaneous burst of applause as Magnus got down from the table and gave Brian a hug.

Brian coughed to clear his throat and carefully placed the picture on the table. "Firstly, I'd just like to thank everyone for making my life here so enjoyable. This place really is like an extended family to me, and I'm very touched that you should throw this impromptu party in my honour. And secondly, I'd just like to correct you, Magnus. This picture is not a limited edition print by the well-known artist Myles Birket Foster."

Magnus looked a touch miffed. "Are you sure, Brian? Have I been diddled?"

Brian laughed. "Not at all. This charming study, Magnus, is an original watercolour by Myles Birket Foster, and I can assure you that whatever you paid for it, wouldn't have been anywhere near enough."

About the Author

Back in the distant mists of time, Alex spent three years at Maidstone College of Art; an establishment that David Hockney once taught at and later described as one of the most miserable episodes of his life. Here, Alex was responsible for producing, among other things, the college's first theatrical production in which the lead character accidentally caught fire. Following college, he found employment in the advertising industry as a copywriter. He has turned to writing fiction in the twilight years of his writing career. His novella, *Sleeping with the Blackbirds* — a black, comic urban fantasy, was initially written for his children and published by Pen Press. It was longlisted by the 2018 Millennium Book Awards and selected the following year by the Indie Author Project for distribution to public libraries across the US and Canada. His thriller *The Chair Man* is set in London following the terrorist attacks in 2005 and was a finalist in The Wishing Shelf Book Awards 2021. *A Brand to Die For* is the first in his Lovejoy & Finkle murder mystery series and is set in the London advertising world of 1983. *One Man Down* is the sequel. Alex possesses an exceptionally poor sense of direction and lives somewhere in North West London with his wife and overindulged cat. He is also quite possibly the only person on the planet to have been inadvertently locked in a record shop on Christmas Eve. His books can be found at all good online retailers, and you can find out more about him and over 100 authors he has interviewed by visiting his website: booksbyalexpearl.weebly.com

ROUNDFIRE
BOOKS

FICTION

Put simply, we publish great stories. Whether it's literary or popular, a gentle tale or a pulsating thriller, the connecting theme in all Roundfire fiction titles is that once you pick them up you won't want to put them down.

If you have enjoyed this book, why not tell other readers by posting a review on your preferred book site.

The Cause
Roderick Vincent
The second American Revolution will be a
fire lit from an internal spark.
Paperback: 978-1-78279-763-0 ebook: 978-1-78279-762-3

Don't Drink and Fly
The Story of Bernice O'Hanlon: Part One
Cathie Devitt
Bernice is a witch living in Glasgow. She loses her way
in her life and wanders off the beaten track looking for the
garden of enlightenment.
Paperback: 978-1-78279-016-7 ebook: 978-1-78279-015-0

Gag
Melissa Unger
One rainy afternoon in a Brooklyn diner, Peter Howland
punctures an egg with his fork. Repulsed, Peter pushes
the plate away and never eats again.
Paperback: 978-1-78279-564-3 ebook: 978-1-78279-563-6

The Master Yeshua
The Undiscovered Gospel of Joseph
Joyce Luck
Jesus is not who you think he is. The year is 75 CE. Joseph
ben Jude is frail and ailing, but he has a prophecy to fulfil ...
Paperback: 978-1-78279-974-0 ebook: 978-1-78279-975-7

On the Far Side, There's a Boy
Paula Coston
Martine Haslett, a thirty-something 1980s woman, plays hard
on the fringes of the London drag club scene until one night
which prompts her to sign up to a charity. She writes to a
young Sri Lankan boy, with consequences far and long.
Paperback: 978-1-78279-574-2 ebook: 978-1-78279-573-5

Tuareg
Alberto Vazquez-Figueroa
With over 5 million copies sold worldwide, *Tuareg* is a classic
adventure story from best-selling author Alberto Vazquez-
Figueroa, about honour, revenge and a clash of cultures.
Paperback: 978-1-84694-192-4

Readers of ebooks can buy or view any of these bestsellers by
clicking on the live link in the title. Most titles are published
in paperback and as an ebook. Paperbacks are available in
traditional bookshops. Both print and ebook formats are
available online.

Find more titles and sign up to our readers' newsletter, visit:
www.collectiveinkbooks.com/fiction

What People Are Saying About

One Man Down and Other Titles by the Author

Pearl has written a very funny and compelling page-turner. 11 out of 10!
Jeremy Dein, KC and presenter of the BBC's award-winning series *Murder, Mystery and My Family*

Alex Pearl breaks all the rules of fashionable modern fiction — meaning that his stories are compelling, his characters are plausible and live in a recognisable world, and his writing is clear, vivid and entertaining.
Jonathan Margolis, columnist and author

Alex Pearl's new novel is a highly entertaining tale of shenanigans and skulduggery set in 1980s London ad land. Pearl is a very funny writer, with a keen eye for the absurdities of life.
Ian Critchley, book reviewer and writer

Many a true word is spoken in jest. And former ad man Alex Pearl gives us plenty of pithy truths, as well as spot-on jests, in this witty exposé of the world of advertising agencies in the supercool '80s. Clever, unsparing, engaging and a lot of fun.
Sue Clark, former comedy writer for the BBC and author of *Note to Boy* and *A Novel Solution*

There's no mistaking excellent work, and Alex Pearl writes excellent stories. Novels that read like great films. Engaging, immersive, relatable. And funny. Leaving me sorry that *One Man Down* is now done, yet eager to read Pearl's next book.
Bill Arnott, bestselling author of the *Gone Viking* travelogues and *The Year of Living Danishly*

In *One Man Down*, Alex Pearl's biting satire on 80s individualism, London's adland is as much a character as Morse's Oxford. Run on two parts alcohol and one part cynicism, the sybaritic excesses of old Soho's creatives are the perfect accompaniment to this feast of theft, blackmail and murder.

Pete Langman, author of *Killing Beauties, Slender Threads, Black Box*, and *The Country House Cricketer*

A 1980s gem sizzling with witty dialogue and the mysterious murders of an advertising executive and a fraudster to boot. Alex Pearl writes from his personal experience of having worked in 'the glory days of British advertising.' Its tongue-in-cheek anecdotes and unashamed name-dropping of celebs like Julian Clary, had me laughing out loud. This is well written, entertaining, and different from the usual murder mystery.

M. J. Mallon, author of the *Curse Of Time* series: *Bloodstone* and *Golden Healer*

The worlds of cricket, advertising, and 1980s London can feel far away if you aren't British. But in Alex Pearl's capable hands they are made real — and very, very witty. Mr. Pearl clearly knows what he's writing about. The pace of the writing is brisk, but you'll want to take your time in order to savor the quips and puns. *One Man Down* is a highly enjoyable read!

Jadi Campbell, 2023 San Francisco Book Festival Winner with *The Trail Back Out*

This book is a great read for anyone who enjoys a nostalgic wallow in memories of the 1980s. The author evokes the detail of office life in the advertising business with pin-sharp precision. His protagonists, a lovable creative team, lead us through a world where real life events and cameo appearances by well known faces from the time give the reader a warm glow of

recognition. Naturally, it's a world where murder is afoot and, whilst the main characters don't take on the detective role one might expect, they are nonetheless essential cogs in a tale that winds up with a satisfyingly unexpected conclusion. Lots of fun and highly recommended.
Review of *A Brand to Die For* by **Chris Chalmers**, author of six novels including *Five to One* and *Fenella's Fair Share*

The louche atmosphere and badinage of the 1980s is wonderfully conveyed by Pearl ... Anyone who wants a fast-paced read will enjoy this book with its unpredictable twists and turns, often darkly comic along the way.
Review of *A Brand to Die For* by **Eleanor Levy**, *Suburb News*

I so enjoyed reading this book. A glorious reminder of the advertising world in the pre-digital 1980s. Such happy memories of the attitudes we had — "below the line, beyond the pale" and so on. And the fun we had too. Alex Pearl's obvious enjoyment of language delights with playful plays on words and witty observations on human behaviour: "the bland leading the bland"; "Shakespearean copywriters getting bard-ons"; "cereal murderers doing porridge" and more. The engaging characters move the plot forward at a fast, easy pace.
Review of *A Brand to Die For* by **Hugh Salmon**, playwright (*Into Battle*)

Vividly written, and brought back many memories of what it was like to be in advertising in London in the '80s. I remember those watering holes well! Great fun and unfolds at a cracking pace.
Review of *A Brand to Die For* by **Peter Wise**, author of *Disturbing the Water*

A perfect book to take on holiday. Apart from a cracking plot, we're given a fascinating insight into the world of advertising. An added bonus — it's very funny!
Review of *A Brand to Die For* by **H. C. Denham**, author of *Almost Human*

I was asked by a young executive creative director recently, "Was it better in the old days?" Honestly, yes. This charming novel is evidence of it.
Review of *A Brand to Die For* by **Patrick Collister**, creative director and media commentator

Just like with *Line of Duty*, I love it when you start getting the back story to a character, then immediately think that they are a key part of the plot. Alex does this with pretty much every person in the book, leading you down several character dead ends and that was a great part of the tale. Just when you think you have cracked someone's role, something crops up to shatter that idea. I would love to know how Alex conducted some of his story research, particularly on aspects such as the terrorist cells, but it's probably best not to ask too much.
Review of *The Chair Man* by **Simon Pinell**, *Forward Magazine*

I don't think people with disabilities are well represented in the thriller genre, which *The Chair Man* goes a good way to addressing ... I'd be giving too much away by going into detail, but this is a fast-paced revenge thriller with some fine action sequences.
Review of *The Chair Man* by **Chris Chalmers**, author of six novels including *Five to One, Light From Other Windows*, and *Fenella's Fair Share*

It is difficult to do this brilliant book justice in a short review. Anyone interested in reflections upon modern society and the

impact of terror attacks, as well as those who simply enjoy a good book, will find this an engaging and involved read. The ending will also surprise them because it is certainly not anticipated.
Review of *The Chair Man* by **T. R. Robinson**, author of *Tears of Innocence*

Michael Hollinghurst is caught up in the 7/7 terrorist attacks in London. He survives but is left paralysed and in a wheelchair, but this doesn't stop him from seeking revenge against those responsible. And it's amazing what he can accomplish with a computer and a dog. The melding of real and fictional events is something I do in my books and I love seeing it in others. What really sells this story is the meticulous attention to detail, both in researching the facts of that fateful day and how terrorist cells operate, but Alex Pearl also goes into incredible detail when he's making stuff up, and that's why it can sometimes be hard to tell where fact ends and fiction begins, and I loved that! The short, sometimes very short, chapters keep the book moving along at a cracking pace without ever sacrificing detail, and much like reading Dan Brown, those short chapters constantly convince you that you always have time for one more. It's a great, original thriller with just a sprinkling of Le Carré, Tom Clancy and Ian Fleming's famous double-O.
Review of *The Chair Man* by **Philip Henry**, author of the *North Coast Bloodlines* series

More than a touch of John Le Carré in this. All aspects of it are incredibly well researched for a start — it truly feels like the author comes from the world of espionage and knows what he's talking about. The plot juggles multiple characters and storylines and moves along at a good rate. What I liked most probably isn't something that would immediately jump out to a reader, but: it's so English. Every time I picked it up again, I was whisked away to the UK ca. 2005/2006 and it was very welcome. I haven't lived there for 10 years now, but it gave me a strong desire to go home.

Review of *The Chair Man* by **Grant Price**, author of *By the Feet of Men*, *Reality Testing* and *Pacific State*

Coupled with my fascination for the colloquial Londoner language, I was fully immersed into Michael Hollinghurst's world by the time the rising action went vertical. The tension grew to the point where I was nervous by the end, and the end was something I did not expect. *The Chair Man* by Alex Pearl is a well-researched and tense novel that I will not soon forget. I would say that Pearl has a new fan.

Review of *The Chair Man* by **Benjamin X. Wretlind**, author of multiple titles in the science fiction, dark fantasy, magic realism, and horror genres

Alex Pearl held me captive from page one. Powerful characters. An incredible plot that typically isn't anything I would read, but was so compelling I couldn't stop reading.

Review of *The Chair Man* by **Dawn Greenfield Ireland**, author of the bestselling *Hot Chocolate* series

A delightful fairy story that deals sensitively and compellingly with real, modern-day issues like homelessness, single mums and abusive parents.

Review of *Sleeping with the Blackbirds* by **George Layton**, actor, screenwriter and author of bestsellers *The Trick*, *The Swap* and *The Fib*

Its wonderful images and thought-provoking scenes moved me to tears.

Review of *Sleeping with the Blackbirds* by **Bramwell Tovey**, Grammy and Juno Award-winning composer, conductor and broadcaster

I devoured this wonderful middle-grade novel in less than 24 hours, and I loved it, though (or perhaps because) it turned out to be far more challenging than I originally thought it would be. Deeper. More profound. Touching on topics such as bullying, intellectual disabilities, illegitimacy, and parents in the prison system, it couldn't be more contemporary, yet it somehow has that old-fashioned feel so beloved by most fantasy readers.

Review of *Sleeping with the Blackbirds* by **Kelly Wittmann**, author of *An Authentic Experience*

Beautifully written, poignant and magical, Alex Pearl's writing style flows with the hand of a seasoned veteran. It pulls you in and never lets go.

Review of *Sleeping with the Blackbirds* by **Patrick Hodges**, author of *Jushua's Island* and *The Bax Mysteries*

I really loved this novel. I laughed out loud multiple times (which I rarely do while reading) and I was very moved at times as well.

Review of *Sleeping with the Blackbirds* by **Valerie Cotnoir**, author of *Your Home is Here*, *The War Within*, *Everlasting* and *Bridget's Journey*

The strength of the author's voice held me captivated long after turning the last page. With the wit of JK Rowling, Alex Pearl has definitely earned his place in the young adult fiction hall of fame.

Review of *Sleeping with the Blackbirds* by **Lisa McCombs**, Readers' Favorite

Alex Pearl has written a tale that is heartening and funny with the appeal of a Twain-like children's adventure.

Review of *Sleeping with the Blackbirds* by **Len Baker**, Suburb News

Alex Pearl deserves great credit for this excellent book. He has spoken to a hundred authors to delve into their working methods. It's very striking that he listens carefully to this wide range of people and allows them to open up as to what makes them tick as writers. The interviews are very interesting — not too long as to be daunting but long enough to learn a lot about each of the authors who took part in the project. It's obvious that Alex was able to make them feel relaxed and listened to and as a consequence they convey fascinating personal insights into the craft of writing. The range is vast from well-known writers to up-and-coming authors. Overall, a great project!

Review of *100 Ways to Write a Book* by **John Traynor**, author of the *Mastering Modern History* series

I was really chuffed to be asked to contribute to this fantastic project, and I wish I'd had this book on my bookshelf not just when I was starting out as a writer but throughout my career. There is so much wisdom here, I'd consider it an essential for new and established writers alike. I also love dipping into it and being surprised by how authors reveal themselves in their conversation with Alex. The variety of tips on how authors market their books alone is worth the book's (considerable!) weight. This is a terrific companion for everyone who writes. The fact that any proceeds from the book will be donated to Pen International (an incredible organisation that does fantastic work globally for writers in dreadful regimes) is commendable.

Review of *100 Ways to Write a Book* by **C. J. Carver**, author of 16 acclaimed novels and winner of the Crime Writers' Association Debut Dagger

The Cause
Roderick Vincent
The second American Revolution will be a
fire lit from an internal spark.
Paperback: 978-1-78279-763-0 ebook: 978-1-78279-762-3

Don't Drink and Fly
The Story of Bernice O'Hanlon: Part One
Cathie Devitt
Bernice is a witch living in Glasgow. She loses her way
in her life and wanders off the beaten track looking for the
garden of enlightenment.
Paperback: 978-1-78279-016-7 ebook: 978-1-78279-015-0

Gag
Melissa Unger
One rainy afternoon in a Brooklyn diner, Peter Howland
punctures an egg with his fork. Repulsed, Peter pushes
the plate away and never eats again.
Paperback: 978-1-78279-564-3 ebook: 978-1-78279-563-6

The Master Yeshua
The Undiscovered Gospel of Joseph
Joyce Luck
Jesus is not who you think he is. The year is 75 CE. Joseph
ben Jude is frail and ailing, but he has a prophecy to fulfil ...
Paperback: 978-1-78279-974-0 ebook: 978-1-78279-975-7

On the Far Side, There's a Boy
Paula Coston
Martine Haslett, a thirty-something 1980s woman, plays hard
on the fringes of the London drag club scene until one night
which prompts her to sign up to a charity. She writes to a
young Sri Lankan boy, with consequences far and long.
Paperback: 978-1-78279-574-2 ebook: 978-1-78279-573-5

Tuareg
Alberto Vazquez-Figueroa
With over 5 million copies sold worldwide, *Tuareg* is a classic
adventure story from best-selling author Alberto Vazquez-
Figueroa, about honour, revenge and a clash of cultures.
Paperback: 978-1-84694-192-4

Readers of ebooks can buy or view any of these bestsellers by
clicking on the live link in the title. Most titles are published
in paperback and as an ebook. Paperbacks are available in
traditional bookshops. Both print and ebook formats are
available online.

Find more titles and sign up to our readers' newsletter, visit:
www.collectiveinkbooks.com/fiction

Printed and bound by CPI Group (UK) Ltd, Croydon, CR0 4YY

07/01/2025

01816805-0001